FARGO — KILLER!

Fargo reacted like a panther, all the old skill and reflexes learned in the prize ring triggered by the movement. He heard Cord's fist rip past his cauliflower ear, dropped into a crouch, as Cord's left came at him, wheeled slightly, went under it and hit Cord in the gut. Cord rocked back, and Fargo shifted balance and came in and hit Cord in the throat. Cord gagged, stepped back off the sandbar into the shallows of the river, and Fargo, following every advantage, came after him.

We will send you a free catalog on request. Any titles not in your local book store can be purchased by mail. Send the price of the book plus 35c shipping charge to Belmont Tower Books, Two Park Avenue, New York, New York 10016.

Titles currently in print are available in quantity for industrial and sales promotion use at reduced rates. Address inquiries to our Promotion Department.

Shotgun
Man

John Benteen

BELMONT TOWER BOOKS • NEW YORK CITY

A BELMONT TOWER BOOK

Published by

Tower Publications, Inc.
Two Park Avenue
New York, N.Y. 10016

Chapter I

His name was Fargo. When he wrote it large in the register of the hotel in Green River, Wyoming, he was aware of the curious, slightly apprehensive eyes of the clerk ranging over him. The old days were gone; this end of southwestern Wyoming was, now, in 1915, pretty well tamed down. It was not often, anymore, that such a man appeared here— one whose trade, unmistakably, was combat.

Even the white shirt, corduroy jacket and matching pants, the kind of garb that might have been worn by a prosperous cattleman or oil-lease shark, could not disguise that. He was too big, carried himself too lightly and alertly, and his ugly face was too hard and sunbrowned and scarred. The battered old Rough Rider hat perched cockily on close-cropped hair gone prematurely silver-white was another tip-off. Its angle seemed to tell the world to go to hell. So did the cool gray eyes, the nose broken more than once, the cauliflower ear. What with his more than six feet of height, wide shoulders, deep chest, narrow waist, and horseman's legs, even a hotel clerk could tell that this man was not to be taken lightly or trifled with, and his manner was respectful. He himself helped Fargo carry the big trunk to the room on the second floor. "Heavy," he panted when they set it down.

"Mining samples," Fargo lied. Actually the trunk was full of weapons and ammunition. He tipped the clerk a silver dollar, locked the door behind the man when he had gone. Then he went to the window and from this height appraised the little town to which the train had brought him a half hour before.

It was bustling, the gateway to the Grand Tetons in the north, to the Colorado River in the south, and shipping point for ranches not only in Wyoming, but in Utah and Colorado. Fargo did not know why he had been summoned here, but it was good to be back in the northwest. He had made a lot of money out of the Mexican Revolution in the past few years, running guns, occasionally hiring out to use them, but for the time being, he had enough of the Coahuila and Sonoran deserts, of rebel factions fighting one another harder than they fought the government they rebelled against, and of darkskinned women and tequila. He liked the Mexicans, liked darkskinned women, liked tequila, too. But he was ready to speak English for a change, drink some bourbon and some rye, and he had already

6

stopped over in Cheyenne for a rendezvous with a girl he knew there whose skin was white as milk and hair as blonde as wheat; and it had been a pleasant change.

He was not, of course, tired of danger. He assumed there was danger in what he had been summoned here to do; the Colonel never called on him for any ordinary job. And that was all right, too. Combat was not only his trade, but his pleasure. In the shadow of death, he felt life surging with superb vitality. Some men were drunkards; his real intoxication came from risk.

Now he shrugged out of the coat, beneath which a .38 Officer's Model Colt revolver rode in a shoulder holster under his left arm. He fished keys from his pocket, opened the trunk, threw back the lid. The first thing he took from it was a fresh bottle of good whiskey. With a hard blow of his palm against its bottom, he started the cork, drew it the rest of the way with strong, white teeth. He drank long and deeply, and then he lit a thin black cigar and savored its smoke. While he unpacked the trunk, he wondered where he would use its contents next.

His earliest memories were of violence. His parents had been brutally murdered by Apaches on their small New Mexican ranch, and it was sheer luck that the Indians, the last Chiricahuas under Geronimo, had overlooked the four-year-old huddled in the barn.

He was taken in by a couple on a neighboring ranch. Not, as it proved, out of charity, but because it was a way to get an extra hired hand for almost nothing. By the time he was twelve, he was working like a slave at jobs that would have taxed a full-grown man and getting only kicks and curses in return. So he left, one night—and never looked back.

His education from then on came in a hard school. He'd punched cows, roughnecked in oil fields, cut big timber in the Northwest, picked up that cauliflower ear as a professional boxer, and once had even served a stint as bouncer in a Louisiana whorehouse when down on his luck. But his true calling was that of soldier and fighting man. He'd realized that in the Spanish-American War, when, as Sergeant of Troop A, First Volunteer American Cavalry, better known as the Rough Riders, he had played his part in building the legend that had helped vault the Regiment's lieutenant-colonel to the Presidency of the United States.

After San Juan Hill, Kettle Hill, El Caney and all the rest, the taste of soldiering lingered in his mouth. A long hitch, then, with the Cavalry in the Philippines during the Insurrection, and then he was ready to go in business for himself.

Even in the first decade of the Twentieth Century, with the West settling down, there was plenty of work for an expert fighting man. One as good as Fargo came high. His motto was, *Go first class or don't go at all.* Nobody in such a trade lived to a ripe old age; for all he knew, the bullet with his name on it rode even now in someone else's cartridge belt. So, liking women, whiskey, games of chance and weapons, he made a lot and spent a lot.

But it was not money that brought him here. He had plenty of that in the trunk to keep him for a spell. It was the urgent summons from the only man he really gave a damn about, the only one who could command his loyalty or give him orders which he would accept without question or inquiry. That man should be along soon, and meanwhile, he told himself, he'd better check his gear. Another drink and he went back to the trunk and began to unload it.

In Fargo's business, there was one cardinal rule, the law of the combat man: *Stop him before he stops you.* Whether you killed an opponent or not was immaterial so long as you put him out of action before he could do you damage. And that was what the shotgun was for.

He lifted it from the trunk, removed it from its special case of chamois skin, and when its cold, blue steel was in his hands, he stroked it as another man might have caressed a woman's flesh, and his eyes held something of the look another man might have cast at a much-loved woman. He was expert with many weapons, but when you came down to it, this was his pet: he was a shotgun man.

A Fox Sterlingworth, twelve-gauge, beautifully ornamented and engraved, it had once been a fowling piece. Fargo had sawed off the extra length of barrels, and now it was a stubby, lethal riot gun with open bores that could each spray nine buckshot in a wide, deadly pattern. A single pellet was enough to kill a deer—or man. All eighteen, from both barrels at once, were like a blast of cannister from a cannon's mouth. At close range, nothing could stand up against it. It was, in fact, the nearest thing to a cannon or a machine gun in its

9

effect that one man could transport easily, on foot or horseback, and Fargo had carried it from Canada to South America, from the Philippines to the Mississippi. It had served him well for years, the foremost tool of his tráde and his most prized possession. Shotguns could be bought anywhere, but this one was irreplaceable. What made it so was the inscription worked into the elaborate engraving on the breech which his hand now traced: *To Neal Fargo gratefully from T. Roosevelt.*

Fargo's thin lips curled in a grin. Only two people in the world knew what he had done to earn this weapon, which had been presented to him years before in the White House in Washington; and the other one would be along most any time now . . .

Meanwhile he checked the weapon's leather sling, slipped it on his right shoulder so that the gun hung stock up, muzzles down, behind his back. It seemed an awkward way for it to ride, but—Fargo hooked his right hand's thumb beneath the sling, twitched it hard. With amazing speed, the sawed-off pivoted, stubby barrels coming up beneath his arm, pointed forward. In the same instant his left hand shot across his body, and there were two dry simultaneous clicks as it tripped both triggers. In that position the gun was upside down, but the beauty of the sawed-off was that position made no difference. Either way, it required no aiming at close range, all you had to do was point and shoot, and you had your man.

Repeating the maneuver twice, Fargo then transferred the gun to his left shoulder, went through the routine thrice more, just as quickly, just as smoothly. He had been born ambidextrous, and that gift of being able to use either hand with equal ease almost doubled his efficiency and more than once had saved his life. This was not idle play, now, but the deadly serious business of limbering up after a train ride, for practice to a gunman was as important as to a violinist or any other kind of artist . . .

The limbering-up done with, Fargo unslung the gun, ran his hand lovingly down its barrels once more, and laid it on the bed. Then he unbuckled the shoulder harness and took a cartridge belt and hip holster from the trunk. Each bullet loop glittered with a fat brass cartridge, and the slug in each was of a special kind—a hollow-point.

Until the Filipino Insurrection, the kind of .38 Fargo transferred from the shoulder holster to the gunbelt had been Army standard issue. But the Moros of Mindanao were like nothing the Army had ever come up against. Mohammedans, ferocious fighters, filled themselves with drugs, bound their loins up with excruciating tightness, and, drunk on religious fervor, went *juramentado*—they ran amok, blindly killing any living thing that crossed their paths. A .38 slug wouldn't stop them; Fargo had seen six poured into a *juramentado* Moro and the man had still killed two of his opponents before he fell.

So the Army had adopted the heavier .45 Colt automatic, which fired more rounds faster and slammed home a heavier slug. It stopped the Moros, but Fargo found it badly balanced and prone to jam. He clung to the old .38, but beefed

11

up its shock-power with hollow-point ammunition. Such a dumdum slug would virtually explode in flesh, ripping a dreadful wound, with shocking power that would stop a grizzly in its tracks. No matter where it struck a man, it tore him up, laid him down, and drained the fight from him. Brutal as such bullets were, they gave Fargo an edge, and such advantages were important.

There was a Winchester rifle, too, in the trunk, a .30-30. An indispensable part of his arsenal, it was an interchangeable one as well. He could not do without a rifle, but he'd owned many Winchesters, and this was just another good and useful tool, with no sentimental value. He checked its action, laid it aside. Then his hand went to his hip pocket. What it brought out was a knife of strange design.

Six inch handles, split and hinged, of water-buffalo horn polished to a high sheen and ridged for better grip, folded down across a ten-inch blade, razor sharp, leaving four inches of point protruding. Called a Batangas knife, it had been made by the incomparable artisans of southern Luzon, specially hardened and tempered so that its point could be driven through a silver dollar with a single blow, without dulling or breaking.

Fargo flipped his hand; a latch came loose, the split-grips fell back into his palm, unsheathing the full length of deadly blade. He dropped into the cold-steel fighter's crouch, made a few passes with his right hand, a few with his left. Then he closed the weapon, slid it in his special sheath, which in turn rode in his hip pocket. He turned again to the trunk and took out the bandoliers.

Heavy leather belts designed to criss-cross his torso, they glinted with ammunition. One held cartridges for the Winchester; the other was stuffed with fat twelve-gauge shells for the sawed-off Fox. They were heavy, but he was accustomed to their weight when they were slung across his body, and they were vital. To run out of ammunition in a fight was to die.

Along with clothes and other gear, there was more ammunition in the trunk. Fargo was fussy about what he fed his weapons, about bullet-weight and powder charges, proper primers, and the like. When possible, he handloaded his own and carried a reserve supply.

In addition to the weapons, there was also about fifteen thousand dollars in currency and gold deep inside the trunk, collected in El Paso from the agent of his best customer, Pancho Villa. Under ordinary circumstances, Fargo would not have worked again until it was gone, blasted in a three-months binge or less of high-rolling: gambling, good whiskey, better women. But these were not ordinary circumstances. If the Colonel wanted him to work, the binge could wait. Fargo restored his weapons to the trunk, save for the Colt and knife, locked its big padlock with its special key. Then he stripped the shirt from his big, bronzed torso, rippling with muscle, puckered and streaked with the scars of many wounds, badges of his trade. He washed off travel dirt, brushed his teeth—he always took good care of them; nothing laid a man lower quicker in a far place than a bad tooth—and, squinting at his face in a ripply mirror, decided he'd shave later.

It was an ugly face, astonishingly so, but he'd long since grown used to it. Nor was it a handicap: its rough-hewn masculinity drew the eyes of women automatically; and it warned men to walk wide around him unless they had urgent business. He put on a fresh shirt, lit another cigar, had another drink, and waited for the Colonel.

He did not have to wait long. Ten minutes, the cigar burned halfway to ash, and someone knocked on the door. Fargo went to it, hand on holstered gun. "Who is it?" he asked, his caution instinctive.

"Sergeant Fargo?"

He recognized the voice, grinned, unlocked the door and opened it; and the Colonel came into the room. Fargo quickly closed and locked the door again and stepped back and looked at the only man he had ever met who was both tougher and smarter than he himself claimed to be.

Chapter II

He had been rancher in the Dakotas, Under-Secretary of the Navy; Vice President and President of the United States. He had led men in combat, forced the construction of the Panama Canal, captained expeditions of exploration through wild and unknown country; and somehow he'd found time, as well, to write a shelf of books and father a lively brood of children. He was a gentleman and fighting man, scholar and cowpuncher, politician and dead shot; and it seemed incredible that so many talents and so much energy and courage could be packed into such a small and dumpy figure. But he moved with an outdoorsman's walk, and his round face with gray mustache, buck teeth, thick glasses, and a ready smile concealed a keen and sometimes ruthless intelligence. He was, in short, all man; in his own way as much man as Neal Fargo and maybe more; and their respect for one another, as well as their admiration, was complete. "Sergeant." The Colonel shook Fargo's hand vigorously. "It's bully to see you again. I was afraid you wouldn't make it."

"I almost didn't. Your letter chased me across hell and half of Mexico before I got it. Colonel, how you doing?"

"Fair, for an old man who's lost a big election." He had been defeated in a third-party bid for another term as President last year. "And probably better, if you can spare a little of that bourbon."

"You shall have it." Fargo used the one cloudy glass the hotel supplied for his guest and drank from the bottle himself as the Colonel, grinning, said: "Cheers."

Then the older man's smile went away. He indicated the outfit he wore: canvas shooting jacket over flannel shirt; riding pants; high boots. "Sergeant, I've got to pull out for the Tetons tomorrow on what's supposed to be an assignment to write an article for a magazine. That's a blind. I needed an excuse to come west and meet you. Everything I do is watched nowadays, reporters following me all over the place. So I'll get directly to the point. I've got a job for you. It's dangerous as sin, maybe the most dangerous thing I've ever asked you to undertake. But—if you survive it—the pay will be good. Interested?"

Fargo drank again, lowered the bottle, grinning. "You make it sound real attractive."

The Colonel's laugh was harsh, scratchy. "I

16

thought you would be." Once more, he sobered. Reaching in his pocket, he took out a thick, folded document which Fargo saw immediately was a map. "Do you know the Colorado River?"

Fargo felt a prickle of excitement. "Nobody really knows the Colorado."

"True. Which is precisely what this is all about." Going to a table, the Colonel spread out the map. "This chart was prepared under the personal supervision, nearly fifty years ago, of Major John Wesley Powell. It's still the most up to date map of the course of the Colorado River that we have. Do you know who Powell was?"

"The first man to explore the Colorado, wasn't he?"

"Right. He was a Union Army veteran, only had one arm, but one of those men nobody could stop. Not long after the Civil War, he led an expedition down the Green to the Colorado and thence through the Grand Canyon of Arizona to the river's mouth in the Gulf of Mexico. Later, Powell founded the U. S. Geological Survey and the Bureau of Ethnology, as well as the Bureau of Reclamation, which has undertaken the responsibility to improve Western farmlands by irrigation and conservation practices."

"Quite a man."

"Indeed. The point is, however, Fargo, that as good as Powell's explorations and measurements were, they were made fifty years ago, with instruments we'd consider primitive. And nobody has really done an up-to-date exploration of the Colorado since."

Fargo said, "I've heard of a couple of boys from Arizona named Kolb who ran the same route."

"Of course. But they were photographers by trade, not scientists or geographers. They added to our knowledge of the river, yes, but not enough."

Pausing, eyes gleaming behind thick lenses, the Colonel tapped the map emphatically with a stubby forefinger. "The Colorado, Fargo! It's one of the major rivers of America and yet so little is really known about it, because it's one of the wildest, fiercest rivers, too. You could say it begins here, with the Green River draining down from Wyoming through Utah, where it meets the Grand, coming in from Colorado to form the real Colorado. After that, it plunges on through canyons big enough to hide the city of Chicago, down rapids that run faster than a locomotive, waterfalls, whirlpools, until eventually it flows into the ocean near Baja California. And it remains untapped, unharnessed and unused."

"There used to be steamboats ran up it from the south as far as Needles, California, I think," Fargo said. "Some placer mining on it, some of it to fair scale, done with dredges. What other uses would you put it to?"

"We can't say, until it's thoroughly explored and surveyed by reliable engineers. But there could be plenty. Fargo, the Colorado is one of the great resources of this country. Billions of gallons of water running squarely through the desert and all going smack to waste! If some of that could be used for irrigation, think what it could mean." The Colonel hit the table with his fist. "But even that's not the main thing! Electricity, Fargo! Electricity is gen-

18

erated by water power—and the Colorado is pure, racing, untamed water power! It could be dammed and put to work—and who knows what changes that would make in the West?"

Fargo said nothing. The Colonel looked at him wryly. "Changes in the West. That idea doesn't appeal to you much, does it?"

Fargo said, "A wolf don't like to see the farmers cut down the woods, if you get my meaning."

"I know. In many ways I feel the same. That's why I worked so hard to set up the National Forest systems when I was President. To keep part of the country wild. Besides, don't worry. I'm not going to put you out of business. There'll always be a job for a man who can use his guns—in your lifetime and mine and likely far into the future. Anyhow, you need to know the background."

He turned, went to the window, looked out wordlessly at the little cowtown's street below. "I built the Panama Canal, Neal, so I guess you could say I'm accustomed to thinking big. The Colorado— the idea of putting it to use has been haunting me. Had I been elected last year, I would have spent government money on a full-scale expedition. Meanwhile, I did spend some money—not government funds—on a smaller one. Do you remember Lieutenant Knight, K Troop, the old regiment?"

Fargo frowned. "Yeah, I remember him. K Troop was all Easterners. We used to laugh at 'em, but they turned out to be as tough as any of us, and Knight was about the toughest of 'em all."

"Right. Well, Harry Knight stayed in the Army, rose to Colonel of Engineers before he retired a few years ago. But he was just as adventurous as ever. Last year, he came to me with a scheme for another expedition down the Colorado, one composed mainly of experienced scientists and engineers. The idea was to survey the river and all its resources completely with modern instruments in the light of modern knowledge. It was to be a preliminary expedition for a full-scale one later on, if I were elected President. With the help of the Explorers Club, the National Geographic Society, and the Smithsonian Institute, plus some wealthy friends, I scraped up the money Knight needed. Last summer he embarked from below Green River with twelve men and four specially constructed boats and a great deal of valuable equipment."

The Colonel broke off. After a moment, he turned, and his eyes were hard as he faced Fargo. "Nothing has been heard from them since, none of them. Fargo, the whole expedition has disappeared completely."

Neal Fargo chewed the black cigar clamped between his teeth. "Maybe the river ate them."

"No." The Colonel's voice was sharp. "Part of them, perhaps. But not the whole expedition. Those boats were a new type, scientifically constructed for the trip and damned near unsinkable. Every man of the crew was experienced on white water, expert outdoorsmen in all other respects. It's unthinkable that the Colorado River could have taken all of them and left no survivors, not one to tell the tale." Carrying his glass, he went to the dresser, poured one more very small drink.

"Sergeant Fargo, I don't think it was the wild river that got Knight's expedition. I think it was the wild men along it."

For a moment Fargo was silent, assessing old rumors and campfire stories. "That's not impossible."

"No, I don't think it is. You talked about wolves and woods a few minutes ago. In a sense, what you said applied to the Colorado in spades. It's wild, remote, and unexplored. You could call it the last big patch of woods for the wolves to hide in—and I think plenty are still hiding there. You know about the Old Outlaw Trail."

"Sure," Fargo said. "Ran from Canada to Mexico. The Owlhoot Trail they called it sometimes. Touched at the Colorado half a dozen different places."

"Exactly." The Colonel went to the map. "The parks and holes and badlands along the Colorado made a fine series of stopovers for badmen on the dodge and rustled stock. Take Brown's Hole, for instance, not far from here, where the Wyoming, Utah and Colorado state lines all come together."

Fargo grinned. "Yeah. In the old days it drove the lawmen crazy. A wanted man could skip back and forth across state lines with no trouble at all. And, of course, there's Robbers Roost, over in the San Rafael country in Utah, not far above the Dandy Crossing."

The Colonel looked at him narrowly. "I won't ask if you've ridden that trail yourself," he said, grinning faintly.

"I've been a lot of places. And I know a lot of

people who have been a lot of others. In the old days . . ."

"The old days," said the Colonel with irony. "Fargo, it's only 1915. You talk as if the West were tame."

"Not where I've been," Fargo said.

"You mean along the border. Well, it's not all that tame in this country, either. It's only been five or six years since Butch Cassidy's Wild Bunch broke up and he and the Sundance Kid were killed down in Bolivia. But . . . until recently there were still plenty of wanted men in circulation. I'll grant you, their pickings have grown thin: bank and train robberies have tapered off and fences have cut down on rustling—but there are still a lot of hard cases who've never been accounted for, men with their pictures still on the post office walls. Some have gone to Mexico or South America, true; some have changed their names and settled down. But others have simply disappeared. And I think you and I both know where they have gone. I think they have holed up along the Colorado. And I think I was a fool to send Knight's expedition down there unprepared to meet them. Because, Fargo, I think there are still plenty of men along that river who would kill to keep their presence there a secret and maintain their hiding places. Men who, the last thing they want is to see the Colorado opened and surveyed and explored. And I blame myself for having sent Knight's team into such a pack of wolves without proper preparation."

He paused. "Anyway, that's the background, Neal. Now. There's a second expedition waiting, hidden, to shove off from downstream on the Green in a week. Its mission is to search for any trace of Knight and his men, as well as carry out certain scientific projects. And I don't want to see it fall prey to the human wolves along the Colorado. It's your job to see that doesn't happen—if you'll take it. And before I have your answer, I'll add this. Bring it off and there's a minimum of fifteen thousand in it for you."

Neal Fargo was silent for a moment. Presently, he said: "I never refused you anything yet. And Knight was a friend of mine in the old regiment. But if the money's out of your pocket, I can't accept it."

"It's not out of mine. I've raised funds from the same sources that financed Knight's group. Included in the budget is the sum for you—*if* you bring back positive proof of the fate of every member of Knight's team, or *if*—"

He broke off.

"If?" Fargo said quietly.

"If any of them are still alive, you'll be expected to find them and bring them back. Rescue them if they're held captive. No matter what you have to do."

"Or," said Fargo, still very quietly, "who I have to kill?"

"Once I gave you a shotgun," the Colonel said.

"I still have it," Fargo answered.

"It was presented to you to be used when needed," the Colonel said. "If Knight and his men are still alive, I want them back. If they're dead, I want justice done."

23

"A tall order," Fargo said.

"Which is why that part of the budget's the biggest. You'll take the job?"

"If I can do it my way."

"You'll have a free hand. That's already been arranged."

"Then, good enough," said Fargo.

"That's bully, simply bully," the Colonel said, and Fargo saw the relief spread across his face. It was obvious that the Colonel's conscience had been riding him. Fargo had never served under an officer who had felt such responsibility for his men, and the Colonel had not changed in that respect over the years. For a moment, the older man turned away. Then he said, "You'll want the details."

"Yeah," Fargo said.

"Very well. Here they are in a nutshell." His voice normally brisk again, the Colonel faced Fargo once more. "First of all, Knight's expedition was totally secret. We decided to do it that way for fear that word that the Colorado was being re-explored might open up a false land boom. You know yourself how many unscrupulous operators would leap at the chance to unload acres of useless badlands on suckers at the least excuse."

"Yeah. And the world is full of suckers."

"I'm afraid you're right. Anyhow, no word of the expedition—or its fate—has ever leaked out. This second expedition will be equally secret, partly for the same reasons, partly not to alert any of the . . . wolves . . . along the river."

"Good," Fargo said.

"Three boats of the same design as Knight's and

24

eight men are waiting at the mouth of Sheep Creek, which comes in from the west, just below Horseshoe Canyon. They were brought in by pack train with all the equipment and assembled on the spot to preserve the secrecy. You'll join them there and as soon as you arrive the expedition will take to the river."

Fargo nodded. "And who's in charge of this outfit?"

"Captain Charles Vane of the Corps of Engineers, who served under Knight for years, volunteered to take overall responsibility. I'm not well acquainted with him myself, but he seems sound, and he's an experienced river man. He was recommended by people in Washington who know about such things. He has overall responsibility for navigation, supply, discipline. But—you are to serve as his co-commander. Vane's authority extends to ordinary operation: you are to take full responsibility for the security of the expedition. Vane knows this, and I have prepared additional orders to him to that effect. For instance, it works like this. If he says run some rapids that you think should be portaged, or vice versa, Vane's word is law. But if you say to stop the expedition because you need to scout, or make camp in a certain place because of danger from human enemies . . . your decision rules."

Fargo frowned. "You said I'd have a free hand."

"You do, when it comes to fighting or to searching out the fate of Knight's men." He paused. "All right, Neal, I know that's not much to your way of thinking. You like to hold all the reins in your own hands. I know, too, that you're a fairly experienced river man yourself: after all, you've been a lumberjack and on log drives. But one man can't do everything, and there'll be plenty to keep you and Vane both busy. As long as you work as a team, you should have no trouble."

Fargo shook his head. "I'm still not crazy about an arrangement like that. But . . . all right, I'll give it a try."

"You'll have to. It can't work any other way. And . . . it will be a personal favor if you bend every effort to work with Vane."

"Put that way, I've no choice. Who else have we got?"

"All picked men, each a specialist, each an expert river man, and each with experience as a fighting man. First, your guide. I selected him myself. His name's Tom Cord, and lately he's been living in Yuma, Arizona. But he's spent years along the Colorado—trapper, miner, cowhand . . . everybody says he knows the river as well as any man."

"I'll size him up," Fargo said. "And keep an eye on him. If he's been along the river that long, he'll probably know who's hiding out there now and where. The question is, which side of the fence will he be on?"

"I expected you to take that attitude. Of course, watch him. He stacks up as hard as nails, but that's the kind of man that's needed. The others . . . well, you'll meet them when you reach Sheep Creek. They cover a pretty wide range. John Michaelson's been a surveyor working on the Alaskan Railroad.

They don't breed soft men up there. Clell Yadkin's a trained geologist, an experienced hardrock miner. He's worked at the homestake in South Dakota and the Benguet on Luzon in the Philippines. Then there are a couple of non-coms from the Corps of Engineers and a sailor from the Coast Guard, his name's Randall. There's a young Zoologist and forester from Oregon named Ward, and a Shevwits Ute who's had a few years in Carlisle Indian School, but who's an expert in survival in the kind of desert and badlands along the river. Nothing has been left to chance; every man, every weapon, every piece of equipment is the best available. Not a man there you wouldn't want to ride the river with—literally speaking."

"We'll see," Fargo said. "Going down the Colorado's riding a different kind of river. But—give me orders to Vane and make them clear; along with him, I have the whip hand, and when it comes to fighting, I'm in charge."

"You shall have them. Can you leave tomorrow to join the party?"

"I'll strike out at sunrise." Suddenly Fargo grinned. "Well, Colonel, I can always leave it to you to cook up somethin'. I figured someday I might have to ride the Old Outlaw Trail. But I never counted on doing it in a boat."

Beneath the thick mustache the bucktoothed mouth grinned. "Neal, good luck. And . . . thank you." He put out his hand. Then he was dead serious. "And remember—I want Knight and his men brought back. Or, if they're dead and there's been foul play . . ."

Fargo said, "Don't worry. Like I told you, I still got the shotgun."

And then, understanding one another totally, they had another drink and spent a long time studying the map.

* * *

Except for the bulkiness of the bedroll carried by the tall sorrel the Colonel had provided, he could have been a cowboy headed back to work after a spree in Green River, as his mount singlefooted out of town just as the sun rose above the barren, yet colorful eastern hills. He had been careful not to attract too much attention to himself; but when Fargo reached the shelter of thick cottonwoods down by the Green River, he tied the horse, unlashed the roll. From it, he took the sawed off shotgun and his bandoliers, as well as the cartridge belt and hip-holster for the Colt. When the bandoliers were crisscrossed over his torso, their massive weight of ammunition seated firmly in place, the Colt strapped around his waist, and the shotgun riding muzzles down on its sling behind his right shoulder, Fargo felt whole and confident again. With a slimmer roll lashed behind the cantle—save for guns and ammunition he always traveled light —he rode on, and now he kept to cover.

That was something he was expert at—avoiding roads and using every bit of shelter and conceal-ment. Considering what lay ahead, it was just as well if such a traveling arsenal did not advertise its presence. He followed draws and gullies, kept off the skyline; and he made good time. He encountered no one except a few cowhands, and he always saw them before they saw him. By nightfall, when he built a nearly smokeless fire, he was in rough country, where it was unlikely that he would meet anyone. Nevertheless, he took no chances, put out the fire as soon as he'd had his coffee, beans and jerky, and when he slept, the shotgun was cradled in his arm beneath his blankets and the Colt was draped around the horn of the saddle he used for a pillow.

Smoking a final cigar and watching the stars wheel overhead, he thought about the assignment he'd just accepted. The Colonel had been right—it was dangerous and doubly dangerous. He wondered if Roosevelt really comprehended completely the risks involved.

First, of course, the river itself. As he had said, no one really knew the Colorado. But the Colonel had not exaggerated in terming it the wildest, fiercest river in the country. You could count on less than the fingers of both hands the number of men who'd survived a trip of any length down that stream; the way Knight's crew had vanished was a fair example. Just staying alive on the water itself, with its endless cascading rapids through vast, sheer-walled canyons where, if you were wrecked, there was no place to come on shore, would take a lot of doing and a lot of luck.

And then, the men. The wolves, Roosevelt had called them, who hid out in the river wilderness. Fargo knew considerably more about those men than he had let on. There were still plenty of old-time gunfighters and desperadoes left alive, and, as civilization closed in on them, they had to find someplace to hide. There were two places in the west which were almost like game preserves for them, the fierce breed which still acknowledged no authority save a faster draw: one was in the wild country along the Rio Grande, and the other was in the even wilder jumble of parks and holes and benches and hidden valleys and sunblasted badlands along the Colorado. From there they could strike out occasionally to rustle horses or lift some cattle, or even rob a bank or train occasionally, though the latter was becoming rare. Mostly, they lay low, hating the modern world that had driven them into exile there and desperate enough for money to kill any passing stranger for his horse, gun, watch or, if he came down river on the water, boat. Surely Knight's expedition would have tempted them; and almost certainly the Colonel was right that men and not the river had claimed their lives. It was damned unlikely, Fargo thought, that Knight or any of his crew still lived. But if they had been murdered—well, he had made a promise and he would keep it. His hand caressed the shotgun.

Then he put out his cigar and slept.

His journey next day, roughly paralleling the river and yet well back from it, took him through country ever more desolate and barren, seemingly devoid of all life save a few scrubby stray cows and an occasional wild burro. Nevertheless, his caution, if anything, doubled. Anybody he did meet in this brutal land of arroyos and wind-carved hills and buttes would not likely be here on honest business. And there was always the possibility of members of the Wild Bunch from the vastnesses down stream drifting up toward settled country to lift some horses or some cattle.

He covered a lot of ground in that day's ride, and the lowering sun was setting the country aflame with orange, red and purple when he decided to call a halt. He had perhaps an hour until darkness, but when you found a water hole out here, you didn't pass it up if it was close to time to camp.

This one was a tiny spring welling into a basin not much bigger than the crown of a Texas hat, but the water was clear and fresh, and its overflow had fostered a pitiful patch of greenery around it. Fargo spotted that green smudge from a distance; immediately, he reined in. In the deep Big Bend of Texas, he would have scouted such a place before riding up, because where there was very little water you were bound to meet whoever traveled in the desert. Such a move here would be every bit as wise. He tied the horse, unslung the shotgun, and went ahead on foot. No coyote could have moved more silently or blended better with the desert, for his khakis had been chosen for that purpose.

It took a little extra time, of course, but a man in Fargo's trade learned patience. What was time when measured against your life? He had no wish to live forever, and no desire to grow old and go out with his boots off. His way of living was to make every minute count and let the threat of death season all sensations—women, drink, food, sleep, and

31

risk—with a tang that nothing else could give. In due time, he knew, he would take his bullet, the one with his name on it—maybe tomorrow, maybe next week or next month or maybe right now. That was all right. But it was a matter of pride not to make things easy for the man who fired it.

He scouted the high ground first, and only when satisfied everything was clear did he go to the water. At the spring, he found only tracks of deer and burros. He drank, splashed face and hair, filled his canteen, brought the horse down and let it drink. After that, he spent some time erasing what sign he and the animal had left in the immediate vicinity of the waterhole. He camped that night on high ground, himself, on the backside of a ridge above the spring. You never camped beside the water, but always well away and above, where you could see who came to it before they saw you.

His caution paid off. About an hour after midnight by the moon and stars, he came awake, sitting straight up in his blankets with the shotgun ready before he even knew what had brought him out of sleep. Then he heard the riders coming.

Soundlessly, he hurried to his own hobbled horse, clamped his hand over its muzzle, held his breath and listened. Three, four men, anyhow, coming to the waterhole. He heard them halt there, drinking, watering their mounts. In the stillness, their voices, even though they kept them low, could be heard clearly.

"All right," one said, after they had used the water. "Mount up and let's move on."

"Damn it, Jim, let's rest a while. We been pushin' hard."

"Can't help it, we got to push harder. It's a long way from here to the Wind River Mountains. We want those horses, we got to be in position two nights from now, and there's no time to waste."

"You ask me," somebody grumbled, "this whole thing's damn foolishness. Too risky. And them Shoshone horses ain't all that good."

The first man said, half in anger, but with patience, as if speaking to a child, "Hell, yes, it's risky. But we got to have some horses, and the Shoshone Reservation's the safest place to lift 'em. We'll have fair cover all the way back."

"Me, I think we ought to tell Dogan to go to hell," the grumbler said.

"*You* tell Dogan to go to hell. I aim to live a while longer. He wants his pay and we got to make a score to pay him, or else he throws us out. Anyhow, maybe we can rake in enough this time to help with that stake for Argentina."

"You're kiddin' yourself. We'll never git a stake for Argentina, not this way. Dogan won't let us. He'll do like he did last time, cheat us, and we'll wind up right back where we started from."

"Maybe, maybe not. Anyhow, we'll at least have a place to lay low. I don't know about you, but I'd rather put up with Dogan than stretch hemp. Now, either you're in it with us or you ain't."

There was silence. Then the grumbler said, "Awright. I reckon I got no choice. All the same, he's makin' slaves out of us. We take all the risks,

33

he gits all the money, and no matter how big a score we make, we end up with nothin' and still in debt to him."

"We'll worry about that later. Right now, we got to get some horses. Move out—and keep your guns up. We're gittin' close to settled country."

No more argument: only the squeak and jingle as they mounted, the sound of hoofbeats drumming, fading into the night. Fargo waited until they could be heard no longer, then released the horse's muzzle. At once, it whinnied; but there was no one but himself now to hear the sound.

Thoughtfully he walked back to his blankets, sat down crosslegged with the shotgun across his knees, and rolled a cigarette. One thing was plain: Roosevelt had been right. There were owlhoot men still holed up in the breaks along the Green and Colorado, and, more than that, the Old Outlaw Trail was still being ridden. A few nights from now, the Shoshones on their reservation in the Wind River Mountains would lose some horses—and the stolen animals would be brought back down along the Outlaw Trail . . . which, for good reason, had also been known as the Horsethief Trail in the old days. Fargo accepted that without surprise; but his mind chewed hard on something else, a name: Dogan.

But that was impossible, he thought. It simply could not be. The man known as Double-Barrel Dogan was dead and had been a good ten years.

Double-Barrel Dogan . . . Fargo's hand caressed the Fox shotgun. A name that once had ranked with those of Sam Bass and Cassidy and the Sundance Kid and the other great train robbers of the West. But Bass and Cassidy had been honest cowboys gone wrong, and train-robbing had been as much high-spirited sport as business with them. Dogan, Sam Dogan, had been another case entirely. Robbery was his business; killing was his sport.

They said that in the stagecoach days Dogan had been a shotgun guard for Wells-Fargo. He'd blasted more than one bandit gang with the sawed-off ten gauge Greener issued to him, and people had learned to let the stages guarded by Double-Barrel Dogan strictly alone. But Wells-Fargo had been miserly with its rewards to him, and Dogan had turned rogue, gone into business for himself. First coaches, then trains, and his technique was brutal and efficient. Dynamite and shotguns were the weapons he used, and he did not care who died as long as he got what the express car carried.

It was all so simple when your disregard for human life was absolute. Pick a deserted stretch of track, wait for the train. Work your timing to a hair, send a rider down, roll a bundle of dynamite, fused and burning, on the track almost beneath the oncoming locomotive, and blow the engine straight up, a technique Fargo had often seen put to use by both the rebel and Federal armies in Mexico. Then your men swarmed over the wrecked train, using shotguns to blast anything that moved, dynamited the express car and the safe, gathered up the loot, and rode like hell, after cutting all telegraph wires. Total destruction of the train and telegraph gave you a headstart of hours, and you had vanished like a wisp of fog long before news of the robbery was in, much less pursuit mounted. You even had time enough to do a good job of wiping out your tracks, so not even the best trailers could follow you.

Fargo ground out the cigarette, lit another.

About six or eight such robberies, though, and Dogan's tactics had backfired. He had become the most wanted man in the West, and his crimes had turned the stomachs of even ordinary owlhooters—women and children had died in the wrecks and under Dogan's shotgun blasts. He was giving train robbers a bad name, so to speak, and the owlhoot had a code of its own. Somebody squealed on Dogan, betrayed him. A special train, loaded with Wyoming State Guardsmen equipped with machine guns, and a volunteer railroad crew, had met Dogan on his final attempt. What happened next had made headlines in every paper in the country in the summer of 1903.

Dogan's man had ridden down and thrown the dynamite, all right, and the engine had been over the explosive and was blown skyhigh. But the train crew had already uncoupled it and jumped, and only the locomotive went as the brakemen stopped the cars. Then, as Dogan's men charged out, shotguns blasting, they were met by a hail of machine gun fire that killed every one of them, their leader included. Fargo himself remembered seeing pictures of Dogan's bullet-riddled body laid out, almost cut to pieces, but with the head intact enough to make identification positive.

So, he thought, finishing the second cigarette. It could not be *that* Dogan, not Double-Barrel Dogan, the men at the spring had cursed. It had to be another one, with the same name. Which, in a way, Fargo mused, was a shame. His hand tightened on the shotgun.

What he felt then was something he often despised, but could not help. It was a kind of sick lust that grew in most men who made their living from their guns, the need to try themselves out, measure themselves, against the best. It was childish, foolish, and yet . . .

Whatever his trade, a real professional always wanted to be the best. That was why rodeos had lately become so popular: if a man could ride or rope, he had the need to measure his skill against others who were good, find out if he were fair, better than fair, or tops. The same urge had drawn all kinds of fighting men to death: it was the plague of the *pistolero* with a reputation. Fargo had suffered from it himself, as his own reputation had grown: would-be and better than would-be gunmen would ride for miles to test themselves against you, if you had a rep. Kill the big man and you became the big man . . . Fargo had been on the other end of the stick for a long time, defending his reputation and on occasion killing men he had never seen before and against whom he'd had no grudge simply because they felt the need to kill him and step into his boots. Colt and knife, he had been up against the best there was.

And yet . . . He looked down at the shotgun.

He knew what he could do with it, needed no reassurance.

But he could not help a brief, sick craving. If, by

some miracle, a shotgun man like Dogan, Double-Barrel Dogan, were still alive . . . a real expert, who knew the weapon as well as Fargo . . .

He spat. Damned foolishness. And besides, Dogan was long dead. It was another Dogan and maybe their trails would never cross and maybe . . .

Still, when he rolled back into his blankets, he was restless.

It was a long time before he got to sleep.

Four days later, he worked his way down out of the Uintah Range, through lonesome, broken country wooded with juniper and bull pine, toward the watercourse called Sheep Creek. He had traveled hard and stayed watchful day and night, which resulted in his encountering no one at all. He had skirted the spectacular Flaming Gorge of the Green, with its nearly thousand-foot walls, and Horseshoe Canyon which lay just below. Now, putting his mount through thick brush along the clear, swift creek, he felt himself being swallowed up by heights towering over him, and presently, at the end of a narrow, massive canyon, he heard a deeper sound than the rippling of the creek: the powerful, masculine rumbling of the fierce current of the Green.

Despite himself, Fargo felt a certain awe as he was dwarfed by the very magnitude of the cliffs that reared above him. He had been in such country before, and yet this hell of cliffs and sheer canyon walls and swirling water had a special quality that was nearly overpowering. But he responded to it, too, in another way, its very size and wildness striking a chord within him. In a way, this was the kind of land in which he felt most at home.

Then he reached a kind of open delta, augmented by sandbars fanning into the stream. First, he saw it through the brush, then he saw movement out there in the open, and he was pretty sure it was the party he was supposed to meet. Nevertheless, when he broke from a willow thicket and into coverless open, the shotgun was unslung and tilted forward across his saddle pommel.

Then he reined in, deftly slinging the Fox across his shoulder. These were the people, all right, with whom he had to ride the river.

They saw him coming, the big man on the sorrel, sunlight glinting on his bandoliers and on the white hair beneath the cocky cavalry hat. Like ants, they swarmed around three beached boats, but they looked up, left their labors. As Fargo heeled the sorrel into a trot, one of the men, clad in military khaki, strode forward to meet him. Fargo saw the silver captain's bars glinting on his shirt. Vane, he thought, Charles Vane, leader of the expedition. As Vane came to meet him, Fargo sized him up warily.

Captain Vane was short, barrel-chested, very muscular, with thick arms and legs and a square, sunburnt face beneath a shock of black hair slightly shot with gray at the temples. His eyes were black, too, hard, direct, even a little challenging. The nose below them was straight and short above a black mustache, neatly trimmed, the mouth thin and short over a craggy chin. Vane's spine was ramrod straight, his carriage every inch that of the professional officer, his stride neatly measured. He carried

39

a holstered Colt automatic on his hip, dangling from a web belt.

Fargo reined in. Vane halted a few yards from the horse, raking his gaze over all the artillery and the man who bore it. His own hand was close to the flap of the Colt's holster.

"You're Captain Vane," Fargo said.

"I am. You'd be Sergeant Fargo."

Vane's voice was brisk, dry, harsh, with an arrogance in it Fargo did not like.

"I'm Neal Fargo," he answered softly. "I've been a civilian a long time. Most people just call me Fargo."

"My understanding was—"

Fargo swung down. "Well, Captain, I don't know what your understanding was or is. But I'm here to join your party, with orders from the Colonel . . . you know who I mean." He looked around the camp on the delta, the drawn-up boats, three tents, a fire sending a cloud of dark smoke straight up. "I thought this jumping off," he said, "was supposed to be a secret."

"It is, of course," Vane snapped, frowning.

"Well, about the only thing you lack's a brass band. You're camped out in the open, you're smoking like a forest fire, and you didn't have a single guard out. Well, I reckon that's my business, to handle that end of it. After all, you're an engineer."

Vane's mouth twisted at one corner. "Sergeant Fargo, are you criticizing me?"

"Like I said, I'm a civilian. And, no. I'm not criticizing. Just taking inventory so to speak." He put out his hand and Vane took it briefly. "Now, let's

40

get that fire out, strike those tents and move 'em back into the brush, and do the same with those boats if they've got to be worked on."

Vane's eyes narrowed. Other men were coming up behind him then. Vane said, "I beg your pardon, Sergeant. I think you're confused. I give the orders here."

Fargo felt a kind of weariness. Well, he had dealt with officers like this before. They were, God knows, all too common in the Army. But he found it hard to understand how Roosevelt could have picked a man to lead this expedition who seemed more concerned with those railroad tracks on his shirt than common sense. He fished a travel-stained envelope from his pocket.

"Well, you'll give some of 'em, Captain. But I give some of 'em, too. Maybe you'd better read these orders from the Colonel before we go any farther."

Vane, eyes fixed on Fargo, took the envelope. Opening it, he unfolded and read the Colonel's letter. Fargo saw the flush mounting beneath his tanned cheeks. Vane evidently read the letter twice, and his hands trembled slightly as he put it back into the envelope. "This is not exactly according to my understanding. I think my orders supersede these. However, I'll analyze them and—" He started to tuck the orders into his pocket.

Fargo said, softly, "Captain, I'd like that back, if you please."

Something flashed in Vane's eyes. "Sergeant, these orders form part of the records of this expedition and are in my keeping."

Fargo sighed. "Captain, those orders are mine and I'm to be directed by them. And I'll say it one more time, don't call me Sergeant. There's one man calls me that when I'm a civilian, no other. My name is Fargo. Neal Fargo. You can use either end, as you please. But if we go down this river together, it's as equals, not a captain and a sergeant."

"Now, you listen," Vane began. "I will not have an enlisted man, former or present—" His eyes met Fargo's and he broke off.

"My orders," Fargo said quietly.

Vane rubbed his mustache. Then, slowly, he handed them back. "I want a copy of them, copied by yourself, at your earliest convenience."

"Glad to oblige, when I get the chance," Fargo said.

Vane's face was almost crimson beneath the tan. "You'll make the chance damned soon."

"I'll make it when I get around to it," Fargo said. "Right now, there's other work to do, and to make sure it gets done, I'm going to read part of these orders aloud to your outfit. I'd appreciate it if you'd get 'em all up here. You can introduce me, and then I want them to know who I am and how much water I draw. We'll get this shebang under cover and discuss the fine points later."

Vane's breath whistled as he let it out. "Now, you wait a minute."

"No. You wait." Fargo's voice was hard, clanging above the river's rush. "I come up all the way from Mexico because the Colonel sent for me. I've ridden this far down the Green. I undertook to do a job for him, and I'll either do it or report back to him why

I couldn't. Either way, I figure he's known me a lot longer and better than he knows you. But if you want to be hard about it, Vane, we'll have it out now. These orders say we share joint command. We consult together. There's times when I can override you and times when you can override me, but we're still equal on this trip. It's a lousy set-up and I'm surprised the Colonel fixed it that way, but maybe he had no choice, or maybe he's been in politics too long. Anyway, I'm not here to lock horns with you, polish your bars, or do anything else except to make sure this expedition meets the goals the Colonel set for it."

He paused. "Make up your mind. Either you agree to observe these orders, or I ride up to Jackson's Hole, find the Colonel, give 'em back to him, and head for Mexico again. The choice is yours."

Vane's eyes shuttled away, came back to work over Fargo's armament. "A gunman," he said. "A professional gunman, like some sort of character out of a cheap dime novel. What could have been in the Colonel's mind to—?"

"I'll tell you what was in his mind," Fargo said. He gestured downstream. "I may be something out of a cheap dime novel, but so are the folks down this river who've been hidin' out here for years and don't want to be disturbed by such as you. Gunmen and horsethieves and bank and train robbers and general killers—maybe they're all out of cheap dime novels, but they're walking around down this river carrying lots of guns and ready to cut your throat for the silver in those bars on your shirt. Your job's to deal with the river, my job's to deal

43

with them. But if you want to take it all on, fine. I reckon you've got lots of combat experience yourself. In the Spanish-American War or the Philippines or somewhere—"

He saw the red leave Vane's face and suddenly he had found the key to the man as Vane's eyes lowered. "Never mind about my experience," Vane rasped. In that instant, Fargo knew that, experienced officer or not, he had never heard a shot fired in anger, and that was something riding Vane. Which did not simplify things at all.

"I do not think it wise at this juncture," Vane said, still not looking at Fargo, "to personally countermand the Colonel's orders. Very well. You shall have your way for the time being. But your performance will be observed and reported on. Remember that."

Fargo said, "Will it, now?" He took out a thin cigar, bit its end and clamped it between his teeth. "All right, Captain Vane. Assemble your men."

They lined up on the muddy flat where Sheep Creek met the Green, and Fargo could almost recognize them from the Colonel's descriptions. Roosevelt had picked a team, all right. Most were young, ranging from middle twenties to early thirties, and they were a hell of a bunch, a good bunch. He understood that he would know them later as persons, for now, all that counted was that they knew who he was. As Vane stood aside, rigid and expressionless, Fargo introduced himself, then read the Colonel's orders.

When he had finished, he said, cold gaze sweeping over them, letting his eyes establish his authority now, "There it is. I'm joint commander of this expedition. There may be some conflicts, but Captain Vane and I'll work those out between ourselves. What you had better get clear right now, if it wasn't clear before, is this:"

He rolled his cigar across his mouth. "Last year, a bunch of men went down this river equipped just like we are, and they vanished. Every man of that expedition was as good as any man here. They were prepared for anything—except to fight. I don't mean the river, they must have fought that. But I'm talking about fighting other men."

Pausing, he saw he had their full attention.

"You may think the edges of the Colorado's uninhabited. Well, it ain't. The Colonel knows and I know that there are people on this river, hard men, fighting men, outlaws on the dodge, that would sooner see a snake than us. Those men are hiding out here because their necks are on the line: if they're discovered, they'll get stretched. They may have killed Knight's expedition to keep that from happening; they may try to kill every man jack of this one. My job is to make sure that don't happen."

He removed the cigar, went on.

"You may know about me, you may not, but the Colonel does. Fightin' is my trade, and that's why he picked me. I'm in charge of the security of this expedition, and I'll lay down my rules about that, and the man who breaks 'em will have to deal with me. I'll guarantee you, if it comes to that, you'd be happier if you drowned. We'll talk about the ins

45

and outs later on and get to know each other better. Right now, this is supposed to be a secret expedition. Let's make sure it is, if it ain't too late. I want that fire put out and those tents struck. You'll make your new camp back in the brush along Sheep Creek, and you'll build just enough fire to cook on, and that from good, dead squaw and driftwood that makes no smoke. You'll pull those boats into the brush, too, until we're ready to shove off. Let's get busy; a little extra work may save a life or two, and that life may be yours, for all you know."

There was, for a moment, silence, save for the rumbling of the river. Then a tall, bulky young man in wet, dirty khakis took a step forward. "Mr. Fargo, my name's Michaelson, and I helped survey the Alaskan Railroad they're building now. I heard about you up there."

"Yeah," Fargo said. "I've spent some time in Alaska and on the Yukon."

"And you left a reputation behind you. Me, I say I'm glad to have you with us. I'd sure rather have you with us than against us."

Fargo grinned. "Obliged, John."

"I'll move my equipment immediately. Everything you say makes sense. Come on, men." He turned to the two Army corporals standing near him.

"A moment, Michaelson," Vane rasped.

They all looked at the captain.

"Those orders aren't official until I've given them," Vane said.

Michaelson's young, rugged, open face seemed to close as his eyes narrowed. "Not the way I understood Fargo's orders. But . . . maybe you'd better hurry up and give some orders, Captain."

Vane's lips compressed. His words were crisp when he spoke, his face colored red again. "My orders are to move camp and the boats into the brush with utmost considerations of concealment and security, immediately. *Sergeant* Fargo will supervise the operation. You will take his orders unless I countermand them. Fargo, see to it." Then he wheeled and stalked off, ramrod straight, to the river's edge, where he stood, looking into the muddy, swift-flowing current.

Fargo's cigar had gone out. He lit it again. "All right," he said. "You heard the captain. Let's get to it."

Chapter III

Now, as the sun painted the gorge with breath-taking colors in its setting, there was no sign of the expedition in the canyon of Sheep Creek, beneath the three towering separate cliffs that reared against the western sky. The tents were hidden in the brush, so were the boats, and the fires were smokeless. Fargo had cached his horse's gear and turned the sorrel loose with a feeling of finality. Like all the others, for better or worse, he was now committed to the river.

Michaelson, who came from Seattle and who, Fargo judged, was all man, helped immensely. He had a natural authority to which the other men responded. Vane stayed clear, remaining near the river's edge, pacing, smoking, occasionally consulting with the guide, Tom Cord.

Cord . . . Fargo made a note to spend some time tonight dealing with Cord. There was a lot about the man he wanted to learn. Cord had stayed clear of the camp-moving operation, mostly hung around Captain Vane, and Fargo had had little chance to size him up, but—

Michaelson's words broke into his thoughts as they stood in the cottonwood grove in which the boats had been concealed. "Aren't they beauties, Fargo?"

"They sure as hell are." Fargo, after years in big timber logging, knew rivers and boats, and he could not help admiring the three craft belonging to the expedition. Built of cedar, more than twenty feet long, with flat bottoms, shallow draught, and a rise at each end, they weighed empty less than five hundred pounds apiece. At bow and stern there were tin-lined, watertight compartments for scientific instruments and perishable equipment and food. Each boat had fourteen inch gunwales, and these were equipped with rowlocks so that each craft could be paddled, poled, or rowed. Big metal eyes on bows and sterns were for ropework, letting them down over rapids or falls. If you had to run a river like the Colorado, Fargo thought, these were the crafts to do it in. But, of course, the Colonel had run bad rivers, and he would have made sure the expedition had nothing but the very best.

"They're a special design," Michaelson went on. "Tested and proved on the Colorado by Galloway and the Kolb Brothers."

Fargo looked at him. "I've heard of the Kolb Brothers, but who's Galloway?"

"Maybe I'd better back up," John Michaelson said. "You know, Major Powell made the first run down the Colorado in 1869. It must have been damned hairy. I know that three men of his party quit cold and tried to walk home, and they were never seen again—the Ute Indians got 'em. But two of the outfit made it all the way to the Gulf of California. Then Powell came back in 1871 and tried again, but he quit down in the Grand Canyon."

"Who else did it?"

"All the way? Not many. After Powell's first expedition, a man named Hook with fifteen miners tried it in 1869, but Hook and another man drowned and they quit. Nobody else tried again until 1889, when a survey party for a railroad tried the run. They lost a lot of men drowned and injured, but a few of them finally made the Gulf of California. Then a man named Stone, with Nathan Galloway guiding, made the run to Needles, California, in 1909. In 1911, a couple of brothers named Kolb built boats on the Galloway design and ran as far as their home in the Grand Canyon, and later one went on to the Gulf of California. And then, of course, there was Knight last year, and God knows what happened to him—"

"We'll find out," Fargo said. "You keep talking about Galloway. Who was he?"

"A trapper who couldn't stay away from this river. He's run most of it alone from time to time, and he worked out his own design for boats. These are based on his . . ."

Fargo, clamping a fresh cigar between his teeth,

said, "I'm surprised the Colonel didn't hire Galloway as a guide."

"Galloway seems to have disappeared temporarily. Our guide's supposed to be the next best thing."

"Cord?"

"He's run the river twice with Galloway, he says. Knows all about it, and so far, he's stacked up good. I don't say I like him personally, but there's no denying he's a river rat. Says he's trapped and prospected all the way from here to Needles, where the rough water ends." Michaelson shrugged. "There aren't very many guides to choose from, and we've got to face it. A lot of expeditions have started, but only a damned few have gotten through." He turned, meeting Fargo's eyes. "Do you really think we'll have trouble with the owlhoot bunch on top of wrestling with the river?"

Fargo said, remembering the men at the spring in the badlands, "Yeah. I think we will. From what you told me, Knight's expedition was the first real scientific expedition since that railroad survey party in 1889. Back then, the Wild Bunch still had plenty of places to hide, Hole in the Wall, Robbers Roost, God knows where else. Those are all cleaned out now. Maybe they let a couple of amateur photographers through a few years ago without botherin' 'em, but when they saw a real scientific expedition coming through to open up the last hideout they had left, they must have hit it hard. They'll be on the lookout now and hit this one hard, too. You ever done any fighting, Michaelson?"

"You don't build a railroad in Alaska without using guns and fists," the young engineer said with a crooked smile. "I've never been to war as such, but I've been blooded. Everybody else has, one way or another, except maybe—" He broke off.

"Vane," Fargo said. "What's his story?"

"Ask him. My guess is he's spent most of his time surveying rivers. And not getting much credit for the risks he's run doing it. It's the combat men who get the promotions, and Vane's over-age in grade. And no decorations for all the times he's taken longer chances in rapids than most men have under fire. He's a little sour, Fargo, yeah. But in most ways he's a good man, except for the weight of those bars he wears."

"We'll see," Fargo said. He glanced at the sky, for it got darker sooner down here in the canyons. "Me, I haven't eaten since daybreak and I'm ready for some supper."

The meal was a river salmon, fat and delicious. Fargo, despite his hunger, ate only enough to almost satisfy him. One thing a fighting man couldn't afford was to be logy with food, ever. He could handle whiskey, immense quantities of it, and still do his job, but a full belly was deadly in a fight. He savored coffee instead, sitting by Michaelson at the campfire and liking what he had learned about the other members of the expedition. He had sized them up and found them sound—except for Cord, Tom Cord, the guide.

He sat at a separate fire, with Vane. Now, as Fargo sipped coffee from a hot tin cup, he looked at Cord through the screen of willows that sealed off Vane's tent and tried to appraise the man. Since he'd had only glimpses of Tom Cord and had exchanged no words with him, that was hard to do. Cord would have to wait 'til later, all two hundred and twenty pounds of his giant frame.

He was, though, Fargo thought, as much like a grizzly as a man. Maybe that came from living in the wilderness. He was huge, blackhaired, balding, with a face like a piece of the cliff's rock chipped off and shaped. His weight was all in muscle with only a tiny overlay of fat, his arms and legs were like tree trunks. He wore a greasy deerskin jacket over a flannel shirt, canvas pants like Fargo's own, Ute moccasins, and a Frontier Model Colt strapped low on his right thigh and a Bowie with a fourteen-inch blade just behind it. He would not be, Fargo judged, a man to trifle with. Which meant nothing in itself, because drawing-room gentlemen weren't much good as guides on a wild river.

Draining the coffee cup, Fargo felt a familiar restlessness. He picked up the shotgun, and slung it as he arose. Michaelson looked at him curiously. "Where're you going?"

"To take a look around," Fargo said. "That's my job."

He made no sound as he slipped through the willows and cottonwoods along the creek. Presently he reached the delta, came out into the open. He heard the rush of the Green River, looked up at the towering canyon walls on the east bank. Above the rim, stars wheeled. *Lower down,* Fargo thought. *We're still too close to towns and telegraphs. If they're there, the wildest part is where they'll be.*

Still, instinctively, he kept to cover as he walked

along the sandbars and the delta, watching the canyon walls upstream and down. He saw nothing alarming and had just turned back toward the woods when he heard it.

He didn't even unsling the shotgun. He only tilted it with a thumb beneath its strap, and the twin barrels swung into aim beneath his right arm and his left hand was ready to pull the trigger. "Who's there?" he rasped, as the rustling came again from the willows.

"Cord," a deep voice said. "Watch that shotgun, Fargo. Without me, this outfit won't even make it to the junction of the Grand."

"Just don't walk up on a man that way. You ought to know better." As Fargo lowered the Fox, Cord joined him on the sandbar. Fargo could smell the musky, rancid odor of the deerskin jacket, the sour taint of Cord's long-accumulated sweat.

"We ain't had much time to get together," Cord said. "Since we're the only ones in the bunch besides the gut-eater that ain't tenderfeet, we better git better acquainted."

"The gut-eater. You mean the Ute."

"Yeah. Jest because an Injun's been to school, that don't mean he's changed none. You wouldn't have another one of them cigars?"

"Sure." Fargo passed one over. Cord lit it, sheltering the match from a waterproof case with a hand as big as a country ham.

He tossed the match into the river. "So," he said, blowing smoke. "You're the great Neal Fargo."

"You've heard of me?"

"Yeah, you're known up here."

Fargo said, "I thought you came from Yuma."

"That's where they hired me on. But I'm a travelin' man myself. All up and down the river. Trapping, prospecting, the like. Ain't much about this old Colorado I don't know."

Fargo hesitated a thoughtful moment. "Then," he said, "maybe you know a man named Dogan."

He could not be sure in the darkness, but it seemed to him Cord's big body stiffened. "Dogan? No, never heard of him . . . Except there used to be a train-robber by that name. But he's dead. Why? What about Dogan?"

"Nothing," Fargo said. "Skip it. Just a rumor."

"Ummm." The cigar glowed as Cord drew on it. "Well, of course, there's all sorts of rumors about this river. Most just pure crap."

"Maybe. What do you think happened to Knight and his expedition? If you spend so much time on the river, maybe you've picked up some information on them."

"Knight? Hell, him and his men all drowned."

"You think that, eh?"

"Know it. Buncha damn fool amateurs. Tried to run it without a guide. Didn't have no sense, no judgment. Got what they deserved."

Fargo said, "I knew Knight in the Rough Riders. Whatever he was, he wasn't a damn fool. And it looks damn peculiar to me. Guide or no guide, I understand he had some good whitewater men with him and his boats were the best. It's hard to figure how they could have all gone under and not a one made it out to report."

"Maybe they didn't all go under. Maybe some

did try to get out. If they did, they got lost in the badlands and died or the Utes killed 'em."

"That's a lie," a voice said harshly from the willows behind them. They both turned as a stocky figure dressed in khaki shirt and bib overalls emerged from the brush. "My people didn't kill them, they aren't murderers."

Cord snorted. "Your people, huh, Birdsong? Listen, I know the Utes. Hell, they might not only have killed 'em, they might have et 'em. You damn Injuns'll eat anything."

Fargo heard a short intake of breath. The young man who stepped into the moonlight wore his hair long, falling to his shoulders in a black shag. His face was high of cheekbone, the color, Fargo had noticed earlier, of an old penny. Clyde Birdsong, he called himself, this Indian in his twenties who had grown up wild in the desert, then been wrenched away from his people, sent to school in the East, and who had been interpreter and clerk in a trading post on the Ouray Reservation before being recruited for the expedition. Fargo saw at once that Birdsong's white man's education had robbed him neither of pride nor fierceness. Although Cord was nearly twice his size, there was no fear in the way Birdsong confronted him.

"Cord," he said. "I've heard that stuff from you ever since we came together here at Sheep Creek. I've had enough. You'll apologize, to me and to my people."

Cord's deep laugh rang in the canyon above the sound of rushing water. "Say I'm sorry to a goddam red nigger? That'll be the day!"

"Why, damn you—" Birdsong stepped back a pace: his hand dropped to a sheathed knife on his hip. Fargo swung in between them.

"Stop it, both of you," he snarled. "Birdsong, you pull that knife, you're in trouble. Cord. You've got a bad mouth. Birdsong's entitled to that apology."

Though Cord outweighed Fargo by more than twenty pounds, their heights were almost exactly the same, and their eyes met levelly. Cord's lips pulled away from yellow teeth. "Say I'm sorry to a Injun? Fargo, you must be crazy."

"Not crazy enough to run a river with two people in the party that hate each other's guts. If there's trouble between the two of you, we'll have it settled here and now, before we shove off."

"What are you, some kinda Injun lover?"

Fargo said, "I've been fighting with Pancho Villa's army. About half of 'em are Indios, yeah. I don't love 'em or hate 'em, but I've seen 'em in action and I respect the hell out of 'em. They're people like any other people, and—that makes no nevermind. This expedition comes first. There ain't room in it for this kind of stuff. Make your apology, Cord; that's an order."

There was a silence, filled only by the cold, incessant rushing of the river through the canyon's high stone walls. Then Cord laughed, and it was not a pleasant sound. "Fargo," he said. "You don't give me orders. I take my orders from Vane, nobody else. When Vane tells me to apologize, maybe, jest maybe, I'll do it."

Fargo sighed tiredly. "Cord, I thought I laid

down the law this afternoon. I'm joint commander of this expedition. You'll take my orders or you'll head back up Sheep Creek right now."

"I will like hell! Don't get too big for your britches, shotgun man, or I'll take that double-barrel away from you and wrop it around your neck!"

"Will you, now?" Fargo said softly.

"Mr. Fargo," Clyde Birdsong said, voice trembling slightly. "Thanks, but I fight my own battles."

"This ain't your battle," Fargo said. He tossed the cigar into the river. "This is a matter of command, of discipline." Deftly, he unslung the shotgun, jacked it open, pocketed the shells. "Hold this, Birdsong."

The Ute took the weapon. Fargo stood there, legs planted, facing Cord. "Now," he said. "You got a Colt and I got a Colt. You got a knife and I got a knife. And you got fists and I got fists. Apologize to Birdsong and tell me you got the chain of command straight or walk out Sheep Creek or decide which one you aim to use."

In the moonlight, he watched the reactions that crossed Cord's face. First, astonishment: then Cord grinned, and it was the smile of a child given exactly what he wanted for Christmas. "You want to fight me?"

"If it takes that to prove you got to take my orders."

Cord spat into the river. "Well, hell," he said, "when I git through with you, you won't give no

59

orders!" Then, in the murk, his big right fist slashed straight for Fargo's face.

Which wasn't there any more. It was what Fargo had expected, and he reacted like a panther, all the old skill and reflexes learned in the prize ring triggered by the movement. He heard Cord's fist rip past his cauliflower ear, dropped into a crouch, as Cord's left came at him, wheeled slightly, went under it and hit Cord in the gut. Cord rocked back, and Fargo shifted balance and came in and hit Cord in the throat. Cord gagged, stepped back off the sandbar into the shallows of the river, and Fargo, following every advantage, came after him.

And would have ended it there if his right boot had not sunk almost to its top in the sand. He was thrown off balance at the river's edge, and then Cord had recovered and as Fargo, anchored, tried to move, sand sucking at his boot, Cord hit him on the jaw.

In his time, Fargo had been kicked by both horses and mules, but Cord's blow was harder. It literally dragged his foot from the sand and lifted him and sprawled him on the bar. Cord came at him, as Fargo tried to rise, dived, and landed on him with crushing impact. Fargo's breath went out, his head rang, but instinctively he seized Cord's body, hugged it to him so tightly the man had no room to move, clamped his legs around Cord's hips. Locked together, they rolled over and over, as Cord got his splayed hand on Fargo's face, fingers searching for the eyes.

"Damn you, shotgun man," Cord husked. Then they had rolled into the river.

They struggled together there in the shallow water at the bar's edge, and as Cord went under, his clawing hand came away just in time from Fargo's eyes. He surged under Fargo like some giant fish, the current did its part, and the two of them revolved, and now it was Fargo under water, pinned there by Cord's massive weight.

He tried to jerk his head up, gasping for air, but Cord's arm forced it down. Fargo let go of Cord, slugged the big man with both hands in the kidneys, to no effect. Cord bore him down and the river rushed coldly over his head, and he knew now that Cord meant to drown him in a foot of water. He had no reserve in his lungs, and what he did must be done quickly. He twisted his head, sank his teeth in Cord's thick wrist below the sleeve. He felt them go through flesh, hit bone. He was aware, vaguely, that Cord howled, and in that instant of pain, Cord's body went briefly slack, and Fargo put all his strength into a roll, teeth still locked, tearing, in Cord's flesh. They wallowed furiously, like stranded whales, and then Fargo was on top and it was Cord beneath him as Fargo came up, released his grip, spat blood—Cord's—and sucked in blessed breath. In that moment, Cord got his left hand between them and with a mighty effort—he had the strength of a moose—lifted Fargo and shoved him back and Fargo came up and fell on the sandbar. Cord reared dripping from the water and came at him, but Fargo was on his feet before the panting bear of a man in his buckskin shirt got to him. Cord's right wrist, torn, poured blood, and Fargo dodged in beneath the left and hit Cord between the eyes. That was his own right, and his left followed. He felt the impact all through his body as it connected solidly with Cord's chin. Cord said something thickly, swayed like a tree cut nearly through. Mercilessly, as his left hand dropped, Fargo finished it. His fists made the sound of a dull ax sinking into hardwood as he rocked Cord's big head back and forth with savage skill. Cord's knees buckled. Fargo hit him one more time, squarely on the jaw. Cord sighed, crumpled to the sand. Fargo stepped back, soaked, panting, bruised. "Gun and knife," he breathed. "Take 'em, Birdsong."

The Ute moved quickly, deftly, shucked Cord's Colt and Bowie from their scabbards. "Mr. Fargo," he said in an awed voice. "You beat the living hell out of him."

"Somebody comes at you," Fargo managed, "that's the only way to go." Then he sat down on the sandbar, exhausted. He was aware of noise behind him, the fight had been heard. Then Michaelson was on one side of him and Captain Vane towering over him on the other. "What the deuce is this?" Vane rasped.

"Shut up," Fargo said, with the last of his breath. "We'll talk about it later. Michaelson, get Cord up to camp and give him first aid. He's got a hand that's gonna hurt him for a while."

"Fargo, I demand an explanation!" Vane snapped, as Michaelson and Birdsong hoisted Cord's inert body, with help from Clell Yadkin, the rangy geologist and mining engineer.

"You'll get it," Fargo panted, "when I get my breath back." He scrambled to his feet. The shotgun lay in the sand; he snatched it up, instinctively cramming two shells from his pocket back into it, hoping they weren't watersoaked. It was good he had not worn his bandolier. He drew his Colt, spun the cylinder to make sure it had not been clogged with sand. Right now, he needed a drink, and there was bourbon in his bedroll. Ignoring Vane, he followed the men carrying Cord's limp body into the willows and cottonwoods that concealed the camp.

* * *

He had his drink, changed clothes—it was chill down here in the canyon by the river—and as Vane buzzed around him like an insect, stripped and cleaned his guns, which he could do in darkness without any trouble, since he could, for that matter, detail strip and clean and reassemble a Colt machine gun or a Lewis gun blindfolded if it came to that. Finally he was ready to talk to Vane. He told the Captain what had happened. "A matter of discipline," he finished flatly. "You ought to be able to understand that."

"I'm responsible for the discipline in this camp. You should have reported it to me."

Fargo raised his head, looked at Vane. "We're both responsible for discipline."

"I am the ranking man here," Vane almost snarled.

Slowly Neal Fargo got to his feet. His voice was curiously mild as he said, "*We* are the ranking men here, Captain. And it's up to us to get along together. Now, I'm going to tell you something, and I

63

think you had better understand it. You are a captain in the United States Army and I am an ex-sergeant, an enlisted man, and that is something you can't stand, sharing command with an enlisted man. So maybe what I will say will make you feel better. First of all, do you know about Samar?"

Vane sucked in breath. "It was the roughest campaign in the Philippines during the Insurrection."

"That's right," Fargo said, "and there's a little custom in the Army that maybe you've forgotten. It was so bad on Samar that the Army thought every man there deserved the Congressional Medal, but couldn't get it for all the survivors. But it honored them in another way. Even right now, when a man, the lowliest private, who was there, walks into a room, every soldier in it, up to full general comes to attention. Maybe you've seen it happen: *Rise, gentlemen; he served on Samar.*"

Vane's voice changed. "You were on Samar?"

"Where," Fargo asked with wry bitterness, "do you think I got this white hair?" Then his teeth gleamed in darkness as his wolfish grin split his face. "When I walk into a room, Captain, it's up to you to come to attention—unless you were there, too."

"I didn't know that. The Colonel didn't tell me."

"Maybe he didn't tell you, either, that I held the rank of General in the Panamanian Revolution that set up the change of government that made it possible to put through the Canal. Maybe he didn't tell you that I hold the rank of Colonel in Pancho Villa's Army of the North. Maybe he didn't tell you that I was offered a field commission as a brevet Major by Pershing if I'd signed up for another hitch in the Cavalry in the Philippines. I turned it down, because I knew there was no future for a mustang officer that hadn't been to West Point in the Army, and because I could make more money on my own hook. But if it's rank that's bothering you—" He bit the end off a cigar. "You name it, I've led it in combat, one little war or another, from a platoon to a division. There's some pretty pieces of paper with lots of official seals in my trunk back in Green River. I'll be glad to let you look at 'em any time."

"Sergeant Far— I mean, Fargo." Vane's voice was a little shaky. "I'm sorry. I didn't know. The . . . the Colonel should have told me."

"The Colonel and I've got an understanding. He don't talk about what I've been up to and I don't talk about what he's been up to. Neither one of us gets the other in trouble that way."

"Well, of course. I . . . this makes everything different. Ser— Fargo. Colonel . . ."

"Try Neal," Fargo said.

"Neal, I'm proud to share command with you."

"And it works the other way," Fargo said. "Me, I didn't have the guts to tough it out in the Army. I always admire a man who did."

Vane was silent for a moment. "Maybe I wasn't so wise. I've spent my whole career running rivers and mapping their courses. They don't give you medals for that, or even promotions. I . . . Neal, it's a hard thing for a soldier to admit. But I have

65

never been tested under fire. I have no combat experience."

Fargo drew deeply on the cigar. "Running a bad river calls for just as much guts. Anyhow, Captain, I've got a hunch that, if it's combat you want, you'll have it before this shindig is over. And likely with the toughest enemy anybody could run up against, the owlhoot bunch. I—" He broke off, as he heard the sound of someone coming through the bush.

Then he recognized the silhouette of Clyde Birdsong, the Ute. "Mr. Fargo. It's Tom Cord."

Fargo said harshly, "What about Tom Cord?"

"One of those soldiers is a medic, he bandaged Cord's arm. Cord's awake now and wants to see you."

"About what?"

Birdsong hesitated. "Well, first of all, he apologized to me. I'm satisfied. Now he says he wants to apologize to you."

Fargo shifted the cigar across his mouth. "Then bring him on."

"I'm already here," Cord's deep voice said as he stepped out of the brush. His big body swayed slightly. "Fargo, I got some crow to eat. You took me, and you took me fair and square. When somebody does that to me, I don't hold a grudge. I'll say it now, hope you'll accept it. I was wrong to badmouth Birdsong and wrong to come at you. I hired on to do a job, and I'll do it. And if you give me orders, I'll see they're carried out."

Fargo looked hard at him, but Cord's face was

66

masked by darkness. "All right," he said. "Apology accepted. We'll forget the whole thing."

"That would pleasure me," Cord said. "Maybe you'd shake hands on it." He put out his left.

Fargo took it. "This ends it, Cord."

"As far as I'm concerned it does."

"Me, too," Fargo said. He let go Cord's hand. The cigar had gone out and he dropped it and ground it underfoot. "Now," he said, "let's all get some sleep. The way I understand it, tomorrow we shove off, and, gentlemen, we've got one hell of a lot of bad river to run before we're through."

Chapter IV

Morning sun rayed down between the canyon walls, and mist rising from the water became a miniature rainbow. And now, Fargo thought, as the men readied the three boats at the mouth of Sheep Creek, it was time to go. The Green, the Grand, the Colorado. Far and lonesome places, challenge, danger. He felt totally alive, full of eagerness as he and Captain Vane held a final conference.

"You and Cord will lead the way," Vane said, "with Birdsong as the third man in the boat. We can't have both commanders in the same craft, and you're the one who has to see any trap before we spring it. I'll follow in the second with Michaelson and Corporal Grant. Clell Yadkin, Corporal Thomas, and Randall from the Coast Guard bring up the rear. If you think we should halt, or if you need time to scout, give the signal. You'll also be responsible for picking places to camp. We have scientific work to do along the way; we'll depend on you to cover us while we do it."

Fargo nodded. "Fair enough. I want each man to be armed at all times, pistol and rifle within his reach, fully loaded. Spare ammo's to be stowed in the watertight compartments."

"Including your bandoliers? You fall in with those on and you're finished."

"Where I go, they go," Fargo said. "I can get out of 'em in a hurry if I have to. Captain Vane, I'm ready if you are."

"Yes," Vane said. His eyes flared with excitement. He turned, looking at the boats fully loaded and waiting at the water's edge. His voice rose above the pounding of the current. "Gentlemen, take your places! Let's shove off!"

Cord took the bow of the first boat, disregarding his wounded, bandaged arm as he picked up a paddle. Fargo seated himself on the center thwart, rifle cradled across his knees, shotgun slung. "Birdsong," he ordered, "put her in!"

The Indian shoved the stern, and the boat floated free, swung downriver. Nimbly, the Ute leaped in, seized his paddle. Behind, the other craft moved out. Then the current of Green River caught them and they were on their way.

It, the rush of water, was like a living thing, and in its grasp the boat was like a young horse on a frosty morning, eager to run. It swept smoothly into midstream and a single deft stroke of Birdsong's paddle lined it properly. Fargo watched the canyon walls above them, eyes sweeping their rims and all the jagged ledges, outcrops, clefts and cracks.

The river here was less than a hundred yards in width, comparatively placid, and blue birds swooped back and forth across it, giving strange ratcheting calls: this was known as Kingfisher Canyon. Fargo, veteran of plenty of white water in his logging and prospecting days, judged they should have no trouble here, but he had memorized the map, and he knew things would be livelier when they left this canyon and entered the next one. Meanwhile, he admired the skill with which Cord set their course, and if the big man's injured wrist hurt him, he gave no sign of it.

They nooned at the end of Kingfisher, made adjustments to the trim of the boats. When they loaded up again, Cord grinned. "Red Canyon, now, and this is where the fun begins."

They shot out into the river, between enormous vermillion cliffs. As the stream narrowed, the boats picked up speed, and now the river's roar had a different timbre, deeper, more sullen and more threatening. Still, it was easy, exhilarating going until, ahead, the canyon made a sharp bend. As they neared that, Fargo slung his rifle, seized his paddle, and as they swung around the turn, he sucked in his breath as he saw what lay ahead.

With express train speed, the Green foamed through a narrow channel studded with rocks like fangs. White water boiled and surged, lashing itself against the boulders; and sunshot mist filled the air. The boat leaped ahead like a spurred Thoroughbred, and now the lives of all of them were in Cord's hands. It was up to him to pick their passage through that swirling, rushing hell, and be right the first time: there would be no second chance.

It was a wild, breathtaking, blood-stirring run. Time after time, the boat's prow seemed hellbent for destruction, aimed straight for a slab of spray-wet stone. Always, at the last instant, the river's flow and deft paddle work swept them around the rock. Sometimes the boat's bow seemed to go clean under, at others it felt as if it leaped into space like a rising trout after a fly. Always it went faster and even faster, fighting free of sucks, side-currents, whirlpools. Cord, Fargo, Birdsong all worked furiously, and there was no time now to worry about ambush. There was only the white, spewing surge of water, the hungry rocks, the blinding spray. It was like riding a wild stallion bareback in a stampede.

Then, from behind, Fargo heard what might have been a shout above the water's thunder. He twisted, saw Vane's boat swing sideways, caught by a suck. It hurtled broadside straight for a jagged barrier of rocks; a second more and it would slam, splinter, maybe sink. At the last minute, from amidships, two long oars lifted like a spider's legs, came down. As their blades bit in, Michaelson leaning hard against the shafts, the boat began to pivot. It swung stern first straight down the current, and Michaelson's muscles bulged as he pulled in the opposite direction, braking, guiding. With an inch to spare, the craft sped by the rocks, reached a stretch of open water. Michaelson dug in with the right oar; again the boat turned and now it was bow first and running on. It was a fine piece of white water work, and the rowlocks and the oars had proved their worth.

Fargo saw all that in tatters. Their own craft was shooting on; racing arrow-straight between two great gray boulders with barely half a foot on either side, it leaped out into space over a yard-high drop, came chopping nose down into the water. Suddenly it was filling, and Cord yelled: "Bail!" Fargo shipped his paddle, seized the bucket at his feet, chained there for such a purpose, worked furiously as more spray added to the six inches sloshing in the bottom of the boat. For a moment, the craft was sluggish, then it lightened as Fargo threw bucketful after bucketful overboard, and, getting the bit in its teeth once more, raced on.

And still the rapids stretched before them endlessly, every foot of passage with its risk, every rock a threat, the near-misses too numerous to count. Fargo's shoulders ached, he was drenched, the Rough Rider hat was sodden, shapeless, and he did not care. He was too full of wild exultancy, excitement. In this moment there was nowhere in the world he would rather have been, no saloon nor woman's bed he would have traded for the thrill of this wild ride.

A full hour passed before it ended. Almost as suddenly as they had taken them, the rapids gave them up. The boats slipped around another bend, and then they were in water comparatively still and

73

slack. Fargo shipped his paddle, unslung the dripping rifle, shook the water from it, checked its action. Cord maneuvered toward a sandbar as the other boats came up. There, briefly, they checked for damage, held a critique of the run. There had been no real trouble, and every man had pulled his weight. "That was a good run, men," Vane said. His face was almost glowing, most of his bitterness gone, now that he was in his element. "A damned good run. If we can make that, we can make anything."

Cord snorted. "Hell, that wasn't nothing. We got water further on makes that look like baby stuff. Wait'll we get past Brown's Hole, day after tomorrow. That's when the real hell starts."

They shoved off, made a short and easy run until Fargo judged twilight to be an hour off. Presently he saw the campsite he wanted, and they put in, dragging all three boats into cover at the mouth of another small creek. Fargo scouted thoroughly, found nothing but the tracks of deer. Then he supervised the building of nearly smokeless fires from driftwood and carefully oiled his guns and dried his ammo. When that, a matter of the highest priority, was taken care of, he went to Cord, who was drying moccasins at a fire. "You and me and Captain Vane need to make a little medicine."

Cord arose, hulking, barefooted, eyes narrowing. "I thought you and me was all straightened out."

"We are, far as I'm concerned. This is something else."

Cord looked relieved. "Be right over. By the way, Fargo, you're a damned good white water man."

"Thanks. You know your stuff, too."

Ten minutes later, he, Vane and Cord sat cross-legged on a tarp. Fargo passed around cigars from a waterproof case. When they were lit, he said, "Cord. I want to know about Brown's Hole and what the river's like." He watched the big man's face, but it remained expressionless as Cord exhaled smoke.

"Why," Cord said, "it's where the river opens out for about forty miles. A big valley, about a day's run downstream—maybe five miles wide and forty long. Current's slow, fairly deep. There's a ferry there. It used to be an outlaw hangout, you know, in the old days, but now there's some ranches in there. They use the ferry to move stock back and forth across the river."

Fargo rolled his cigar across his mouth. "Used to be. What about now?"

Cord frowned. "Fargo, what you driving at?"

"What I'm driving at," Fargo said, "is that I aim to pay Brown's Hole a visit. See if I can pick up any information about Knight and his men. I want to know what I'm walking into when I do."

Vane shifted on the tarp. "Wait a minute, Fargo. This expedition's supposed to be secret. You can't just walk in there and announce our presence."

"I don't figure to. Cord, you haven't answered my question. What kind of people live there now?"

"It's been a year since I was there. Just ordinary ranchers, near as I can tell. Fargo, I'm with the Captain. I don't see no use for you to go there, and I don't see how you can without tippin' off the fact that we're on the river."

Fargo stood up, looking down at the other two. "Listen. I hired on to find out what I can about Knight. I'll never learn anything just by sticking to the river, looking at all these cliffs. Wherever I find people, I got to talk to them. Now, Knight put in about where we did, as I understand it. He had to pass Brown's Hole, too, forty miles of open country, you say, and ranchers there. They're bound to have seen an expedition the size of his, and yet, there's never been a peep out of that place about 'em, for all the Colonel's scrabblin' for information. If it's full of ordinary, law-abidin' ranchers, that don't stack up at all. I'm goin' to Brown's Hole and see what I can learn, and the methods I'll use'll be my own. What I want to know, Cord, is this—can you slip this outfit by the Hole in darkness, so it won't be spotted."

Cord frowned. "Well, that's a tall order."

"Is it? You said the water was good. A riverman like you ought to be able to take this outfit past, make forty miles or so in a night, pushing hard, and find a place downstream to hole up until I join you."

"Well . . ." Cord rubbed his chin. "I reckon it could be done."

"It will be done, if that's what Fargo wants," Vane said firmly. "Neal, I'll see to it."

Fargo grinned. "Thanks, Captain," he said. "Because that's what Fargo wants." Then he sobered, sat down again. "Listen. Here's what I got in mind."

A day later, the sun, at zenith, beat directly down into the canyon, merciless as a sledgehammer. The wet, bedraggled man on the crude raft of cottonwood logs lashed with rope and vines suffered in the heat, as he poled the precarious craft downriver. It was, Fargo thought, a hell of a way to travel, but no worse than riding a drive of logs on the spring freshet on the Columbia. Anyone without that hard experience might have cracked up the raft or gone off it long ago, but Fargo, barefooted, with his boots slung around his neck, rode it as easily as he would ride a horse. Drowning, anyhow, was the least of his worries at the moment, considering the odds he might shortly be facing.

Well, he thought, lighting a cigar, he had done everything he could to put them on his side. The boats were well-hidden upstream; tonight, they would make their long, hard run, and with luck be well past Brown's Hole by daybreak and once more in concealment. If he was lucky, he would join them within twenty-four hours. They had orders to wait for three days, though, if necessary, and to stay under cover the whole time. "Because," as he had told Vane, "if I'm not back in three days, I won't be back at all."

Now, the canyon walls were dropping, the current slowing. According to the guide and to the maps, he should soon be able to make a landing. He sat down crosslegged on the raft, adjusted the shotgun that rode muzzles down on his right shoulder under the boots. He had left his rifle with the boats, and maybe that was a wrong move, but given a choice of weapons, he had to have the Fox. That, his Colt, and the Batangas knife, should be enough. Much more and his story would not stand up.

And maybe, he told himself, this was a wild goose chase. Maybe Brown's Hole was clean, now, inhabited only by honest ranchers, as Tom Cord had claimed. On the other hand . . . He thought about the four men he'd overheard at the waterhole. If, say, they had made their score at the Shoshone Reservation, they'd need some place to stop over, rest the rustled horses. What better place than the Hole? If rustling was still going on, Brown's Hole had to play a part in it. And Dogan . . . Double-Barrel Dogan was dead, of course. But there was another Dogan and . . .

Fargo never jumped at conclusions. He would see what he would see, play it by ear. He finished his cigar and threw it in the river. As he carefully regained his feet, the raft rocking under him, and picked up his pole, the last height of canyon on the east bank dwindled. The river turned, and all at once he was in open country, where he could see for miles.

Brown's Hole. It stretched away on his left, lush meadows behind the cottonwoods at the water's edge, and, in the distance, rolling, rocky hills clad with juniper and bunch grass. On the horizon at the valley's farther side, rugged mountains seemed pasted against the summer sky's almost painful blue. Those mountains hemmed in the Hole, cut it off from the outside world, made it a fine, lost, remote hiding place. The question was, who was hiding there and what did they know about Colonel Knight?

Fargo checked the shotgun, then poled the raft closer to shore. He worked down a margin of willows and other brush that edged a bottomland of cottonwoods. Presently, ahead, he saw the cable of a ferry, running from bank to bank, and the big, flat, wooden craft anchored there, where a road ran up from the river into the Hole. Fargo sank the pole into the water and made for the ferry landing.

Long before he reached it, he saw the men with rifles.

Two of them, in range clothes, carrying Winchesters, they stood on the anchored ferry, one watching up the stream, the other facing down. And Fargo's pulse quickened. He had the same sensation a miner would have felt, finding the first trace of pay-dirt in a place where he had guessed it must exist. As the upstream watcher caught sight of him and raised his gun, Fargo took off the cavalry hat and waved it frantically. Then, working hard, he poled the raft inshore.

By the time it bumped against the ferry, both of them had him covered. One was tall and very thin, with a fringe of coppery beard and eyes like freshly moulded rifle balls. The other was short and blocky, with a drooping black mustache, a knife-scar twisting down his face from eye to chin. Neither, Fargo thought, looked like the kind you'd turn your back on in an alley. He raised his hands as the raft grounded on the mud beside the ferry. "Hey, don't shoot. I'm half dead already. Boy, am I glad to see you hombres."

The man with bullet eyes said, "Keep those hands up, friend, and come up here." They looked him over, taking in ugly face, cauliflower ear, powerful body, and gear that looked as if it had been through a lot, for his clothes were torn, crusted with sand, shapeless from soaking. And they followed him with the guns as he climbed up on the ferry. "Now," Bulleteyes said. "Who the hell are you and what are you doin' here?"

"Who I am is my own business," Fargo said. "And . . ." He decided to take the long chance. "I'm looking for Dogan."

Both men stiffened. Then the man with bullet eyes said, "Billy. Take that shotgun and anything else he's got can hurt a man. Big Ugly, stand loose."

"All right," Fargo said. "But this *is* Brown's Hole, ain't it?"

Neither answered. The man with the scar, Billy, pulled the shotgun off his shoulder, whisked the Colt from holster and thrust it in his waistband. He frisked Fargo, found the Batangas knife. "Hey, Lew. Look at this."

"Hang on to it," Lew said. "All right, stranger. Move out, slow and easy. Up the road."

"You taking me to Dogan?"

"I'm taking you to Garfield. You can explain yourself to him. What he does with you after that is your own affair. Put on your boots and hit the dirt."

* * *

Fargo was cool as he drew on his boots, despite the pair of Winchesters trained on him. Indeed, he

80

even felt a certain satisfaction. Depending on what he'd found in Brown's Hole—honest ranchers or men like this—he'd had two different approaches laid out. Well, he was pretty sure these two had never struck an honest lick since they'd reached manhood, and they had taken the name Dogan in their stride. So, by putting his head in the lion's mouth, he'd learned something, and he intended to learn more. And then, if he were smart and tough enough, he'd find some way to jerk his head out again before the lion's jaws snapped shut. That, after all, was his business.

With his boots on, he marched up the road ahead of his captors. Above the ferry, two horses were tethered. Keeping him covered, they mounted, rode at a walk behind him as he climbed a rise that led from the river. His docility was complete, but every sense was alert. And he heard Lew, who had the shotgun, tell Billy, "This is one hell of a fine weapon. I might just keep it for myself."

Billy snorted. "You'll play hell. You know damn well who'll wind up with that."

"Maybe," Lew said.

"No maybe about it when Garfield sees it. And you'd better not hold out on him, neither. Especially now, when he's just took the Old Man's daughter—"

"Just shut up and watch that ugly cuss," Lew snapped. After that, they quit talking.

As Fargo climbed the rise, the cottonwoods fell away below. Now there were lush lowland meadows, dotted with grazing stock, cattle and horses both. As they passed three fine geldings, bred, he guessed, by remount stallions, grazing near the road, he saw that each of the three bore a different brand. That told him something else. After that, he watched only the terrain, committing it to memory: meadows, bunchgrass hills, mountains in the distance, a few scattered cabins badly needing repairs . . . Then the land was level, and where a cottonwood grove cast its shade, there were five or six shacks clustered around a bigger building like chicks around a hen. Although the larger structure bore no signs, it had been built, Fargo guessed, as saloon and general store; and a few horses were tethered at the rack outside.

His captors marched him up the porch, after they had swung down and tied their own mounts. He entered a big room, comparatively cool, with a bar well stocked and shelves of staple goods: beans, flour, coffee, and other simple groceries. There were three or four tables, too, and a quartet of dusty men sat at one, drinking whiskey. They stared at Fargo and the men behind him, and one who had been speaking let his words trail off. Fargo caught only a tatter of a sentence: "Damn Shoshones could trail a fly across a window . . ." But he was pretty sure he knew who those four men were.

There was no one behind the counter. Lew turned to the men at the table. "Where's Garfield?"

One gave a highpitched laugh. "Where you think, now he's a married man. Takin' his . . . siesta." The others laughed too.

"Shut up," Lew said. "Billy, watch this hairpin." He went behind the bar, hammered on a door there with the butt of Fargo's shotgun. Fargo heard a

82

sound like the growling of a bear from within. "It's Lew," the man with bullet-eyes called out. "We caught a stranger. You better come and see him."

Again that growl. Lew turned away, a strange look on his face. "He ain't happy, but he'll be out in a minute. Meantime, Big Ugly, you stand fast."

Fargo said, "I'll stand fast, but I could sure use a drink. Why don't I buy one of those bottles and let's have a round?"

Lew and Billy looked at one another. Then Billy said, "You got twenty dollars?"

Fargo said, "Don't shoot me, I'm just fishing." He reached in his pocket, dropped a double eagle on the bar. Billy licked his lips, went behind the counter, picked a bottle, pulled its cork, set out three glasses. He poured them, shoved one to Fargo.

Fargo drank, poured another shot and drank again. The trip downriver on the raft had been strenuous, and he needed that much whiskey, knowing it would not hurt his reflexes. Then he thought of something. "Don't I git some change from the twenty?"

"Not in Brown's Hole," Lew said with a touch of bitterness. "That's what a jug costs here." He poured himself another drink.

"Judas," Fargo began. "I never paid twenty bucks for a quart before—" He broke off as the door behind the bar scraped open, and then he stared at the man who emerged.

Three hundred pounds, Fargo guessed. Garfield, if this were he, weighed that much or close to it, a shambling blob of flesh, naked to the waist, pale flesh sweating and repulsive. His head was round as a ball, furred with thin red hair, his jowls hung and dangled and he had three chins. His belly bulged enormously, and the gunbelt around it from which dangled a pair of Colts was twice the size of a normal man's. His eyes were like black currants set in dough, his nose a blob, his lips red, the lower one slack and wet. Clad only in Levis and his Colts, barefooted, he turned Fargo's stomach, but Fargo showed no sign of that as those berry-sized eyes raked over him.

"Garfield," Lew said. "We caught this jigger comin' down the river on a thrown-together raft, looked like the breakin' up of a hard winter. He was totin' a sawed-off shotgun—" he laid it on the bar "—a .38 Colt, and this funny lookin' knife."

"So," Garfield said, an expulsion of breath that sent spittle flying. "Lemme see that shotgun." Ignoring Fargo, he picked up the Fox, examined it carefully. "I'll take this and the other stuff."

"Garfield," Lew said, "I took it off him. I want that shotgun."

"I don't give a damn what you want," Garfield rumbled. "You know where this Fox goes. Look at that fine engravin'. You think *he'd* let somebody else have it?"

"I want it," Lew insisted. "I'm entitled to it." He started to pick up the gun, and then Garfield moved.

It was incredible that a man so squat and heavy could be so fast. One big, thickfingered hand shot out, ripped the Fox from Lew's grasp. In the same

84

gesture, Garfield swung the gun and the stock slammed against Lew's jaw and Lew went back against the bar. Then Garfield had the gun under his left arm and his right hand held a Colt, and Fargo had not seen him draw it. "French," Garfield rasped, "I'm damned tired of you. Make up your mind. Either you get back on guard and mind what I say or we throw you out and you take your chances with a Utah firin' squad."

Lew rubbed his chin where the shotgun stock had slammed it. Fargo saw the flicker of fear in his bullet eyes. "Jesus, Garfield, I didn't mean no harm—"

"Just watch yourself," Garfield growled. "You hear? Just watch yourself, or you'll wind up with a blindfold on your eyes. Now you and Billy both, git back down to that ferry. I'll handle this scissorbill —and his artillery."

"Yes, sir, Mr. Garfield," Billy said promptly. "Come on, Lew." He grabbed the other by the arm and led him out. Meanwhile, Garfield swung the Colt to cover Fargo.

"Now," he said. "I see you bought a bottle. You and me'll drink it and we'll do some talkin'. Sit down at that table over yonder—" he motioned to a vacant one "—and be damned sure you don't break bad. Because I might miss the second time, but I never do the first one."

Fargo only grinned. "And me, I never buck a lock." He picked up the bottle, two glasses and went to the table.

Meanwhile, Garfield had checked the shotgun and found it loaded. He snapped it shut, and as

Fargo sat down, sheathed his Colt, tilted the Fox forward, and wedged his bulk into a chair. "I reckon you know well enough what this gun will do. I'll make it if you don't satisfy my curiosity."

Fargo poured two drinks, aware of the eyes of the four men at the other table on him. Before he could speak, Garfield had drained his glass and filled it and drained it again. He smacked thick red lips. "Now, what's your name?"

"Neal Fargo."

"I ain't surprised," Garfield said. "Not after I seen this sawed-off and that funny knife. I've heard of you. Mexico, lately, ain't it. Runnin' guns to Villa?"

"For a place this far back, you hear a lot," Fargo said.

"Our business is knowin' who is who and what is what. And one of the things I didn't know is that you were in this part of the country. How come you here?"

"Well, I shot a U.S. Marshal," Fargo said bluntly.

Garfield poured another drink. "Did you, now? Kill him?"

"I don't know," said Fargo, grinning. "He had a funny little round hole in him when he fell down."

That amused Garfield, and his laugh was bubblous, but his eyes never changed. "Where did all this happen?" he asked, wiping spit from his face and draining another glassful.

"Green River," Fargo said, matter-of-factly. "I got tired of Mexico and come north. Hit Wyoming and found out there was Federal warrants out

86

against me for smuggling. I heard some talk in Cheyenne of a man named Dogan down the Green or on the Colorado, thought he might hide me out—"

"Who'd you hear that from?"

"Somebody I met on the road," Fargo said. "Let it go at that. Anyhow, I headed for Green River, figured I'd drift down here to take the heat off, lay low, Dogan or no. But the Marshals caught up with me there and we had an upscuttle and I put one down. Then I ran, stole a boat. It was night and I didn't have time to pick and choose. It wasn't much. Came down the river, smashed up in the canyon, damn near drowned. Made it to a sandbar, built a raft, finally managed to get this far. Garfield, I ain't et in two days, I'm whipped and on the run. I need a place to hide. Brown's Hole would do just fine. Or any other place where I can disappear."

This time Garfield did not bother with the glass, drank from the bottle in enormous swallows. He set it down, leaned forward, pale flesh flopping, stared at Fargo. "Maybe, maybe not," he said. "You got money?"

"Two hundred dollars," Fargo said.

"That'll buy you ten days," Garfield said. "Food and booze is extra. You git five days behind, you go on the books. But we charge a hundred per cent interest on the books."

Fargo leaned back. "Now, wait a minute."

"No, you wait. This is what you get. A place to hide where no law can touch you. A warnin' system up and down this whole river, from here to below

87

the Grand. And if anybody comes after you, they got to fight. Nobody'll take you here or in the other place. Dogan guarantees that."

"For that kind of money, he'd damned well better. If Dogan comes that high, he'd better be somebody special."

"Oh, he's somebody special, all right," Garfield said, and picked up the bottle and nearly drained it. "He's real special. He's Double-Barrel Dogan."

Chapter V

Fargo felt no real surprise, somehow, but he did feel a wild excitement and surge of curiosity that he masked. "Don't hand me that crap," he said. "I won't pay that kind of price for it. They killed Double-Barrel Dogan years ago."

"What they think they did and what they did is two different things," Garfield said. "But a man like Dogan don't die that easy. It's Double-Barrel Dogan himself that you're under the protection of if you hole in here. You pay what he charges, he'll see no lawman ever lays a finger on you. You fall too far behind, we throw you out in the cold cruel world to hang. We might even turn you in for the reward ourselves; we get a lot of money that way when folks get in arrears. But as long as you treat us square and pay your rent, we'll treat you square.

Of course, there's one little thing I ought to tell you. We've had spies in here from time to time. None of 'em ever got out alive. What we do with 'em is kill 'em, slit their bellies, stuff in rocks, and sink 'em in the river. If you're a spy, you got to count on that."

Fargo said, "I am not a spy."

"We'll know soon enough. Now, you want in or out?"

Fargo said, "I got to think—"

Garfield shoved back his chair, popped his fat rump out of it, and now the shotgun was aimed squarely at Fargo. "Man, your thinking time run out when you hit the river. I'll buy your story if you shell out, and you better hope Dogan buys it, too. Now, you either pay something in advance or I get rid of you by pullin' these triggers. I ain't in a mood to palaver. I got me a new woman and she's waitin' in the other room." His red lips lifted in a kind of smirk. "Dogan's daughter. You don't keep a gal like that hung up while you talk. You want in?"

Fargo looked into the threatening bores of his own shotgun. "I want in," he said. "A hundred bucks worth, anyhow." He brought five double eagles from his pocket, laid them on the table, and Garfield scooped them up.

"Five days," Garfield said.

"And my weapons back."

"Not all of 'em," Garfield answered. "You get the Colt and knife, but the shotgun stays with me. It's a present for Mr. Dogan."

Fargo half came out of his chair. "Damn it, Garfield, that's my gun."

"Not any more. Mr. Dogan does admire good shotguns. We'll give you two days on the books for this one, Fargo."

"Two days on—"

"Be glad of that much." Garfield's eyes were almost lost in fat as they narrowed. "There's another thing about the way we work, Fargo. Anybody kicks up a fuss, all the rest come down on him and lay him out. Mr. Dogan's rules. You break bad, you'll have twenty men against you in no time. The way Double-Barrel Dogan works, either you're with him, in which case you pay your money and live a long time, or you're again' him. When somebody is again' him, everybody else has got to be with him. They watch each other, Fargo, to make sure they don't screw each other up. You understand?"

"I understand, but I still want my shotgun."

"You should have brought a rifle. Dogan don't give a damn about rifles, but he's a fool for shotguns."

"Where is he? I want to talk to him."

Garfield laughed. "A long way off, where you can't find him unless he wants to see you. I'm his major-domo in Brown's Hole and what I say goes. You think I'm lyin', that I ain't his number one man?" His voice was boastful. "Well, that woman I got in yonder is his daughter. That's how *I* stand with him." He jerked his head. "Anyhow, he gets the shotgun and you can have that .38 and knife back. You pay for what you get and you get what you pay for and not a damn bit more or less. And you watch your step until we're sure how you stack up." Still carrying Fargo's shotgun, he waddled around behind the bar and went into the other room, closing the door behind himself.

Fargo stared at it for a moment, and then he went to the bar and picked up pistol and knife. As he sheathed them both, one of the four horse-thieves at the table said, "Well, fella, you've just heard the gospel. Welcome to Hell."

"Hell?" Fargo raised a brow.

"Once you git in, you can't git out again. Lemme give you some advice, don't ever go on the books with Dogan. You do, you're like a sharecropper back in Mississippi, where I come from when I was a kid. No matter how much you pay, you don't get outta debt. And you try to skip, Dogan'll either turn you in or have you hunted down and killed."

Fargo took out a cigar. "I still don't believe it's really Double-Barrel Dogan. Blame it, I've seen pictures of him layin' dead."

Another of the quartet laughed. "You don't know how slick Dogan is. That wasn't him—that was his brother."

"His brother?"

"Right. And it was Dogan set him and his own gang up to die. His outfit, way I heard it, was quarrelin' about the split. Meantime, his brother had come up from Texas, wanted to join with him. Younger, a coupla years, looked a lot like Double-Barrel. Dogan was tipped off about the ambush they set up on that train, but he didn't tell the others. Sent 'em right to their deaths, includin' his own brother, and it worked out just like he figured—he kept all the loot they'd raked in, his brother got scragged and identified as him, and he was in the clear."

"Man, that's cold," Fargo said.

"They don't come any colder'n Dogan. A man that'd turn his own daughter over to a slob like Garfield—"

"She's jest his stepdaughter," another said. "He spotted her mother when he come to Brown's Hole about ten years ago. She was a rancher's wife—this place had started to fill up with ranchers then. He decided he wanted her, plugged her old man, took her and her kid. Then Garfield decided he wanted the girl, asked Dogan for her and he just gave her to him. It's enough to turn an honest horse thief's stomach."

A man was behind the bar, now, and Fargo fished out another double eagle, bought a bottle, though there was still whiskey in the other; he did not feel like drinking after Garfield. He uncorked it, sat down with the horse thieves. They had heard of him; about their own names, they were cagy and he didn't ask.

Letting the bottle make a round, he said, "Help yourself. I ain't sure what I've walked into. I need a hide-out, but I didn't figure on payin' my shotgun for it."

"Let that sawed-off go, it ain't worth your life." The horse-thieves drank deeply and one went on. "If your neck's subject to stretchin', this is the best hide-out you'll ever find. Dogan came in here ten years ago with his shotgun and some rawhide men and chased all the honest ranchers out along the river. Now he damn near owns the breaks from here to the Grand Canyon. Sure, he's a goddam slave-driver, keeps you hoppin' to score to pay him, and he makes more than he ever could robbin' trains. But, rough as it is, it's better than dancin' on air. Anyhow, you can't buck the system. Buck that, you got to buck Garfield, and even if you get past him, there's always Dogan and that damned shotgun of his, and he's death on wheels."

"Big man with a shotgun," Fargo said.

"They don't come no bigger."

"Well," Fargo said. "In case I wanted to buy my own riot gun back, where'd I apply?"

"A long way from here, friend," a horse-thief said. "Brown's Hole serves the north; Garfield runs it. Dogan's got another layout just above the Arizona line serves the south, Texas and all. Near the Kaibab Plateau, a hole back behind what they used to call the Crossing of the Fathers. It's twice as full of hard men as this place, and there ain't no way to git to it anyhow without swinging south and coming up, less you want to run the river. Let Garfield have your shotgun and relax."

"Maybe," Fargo said.

One of the horse rustlers looked at him keenly. "Friend, you got an unsettled manner. We don't want to be mixed up in nothin' that concerns you. Come on, boys. We've had enough excitement for a while. Let's head for our shack."

They went out, not bad men, Fargo knew, in the sense of being vicious, but, like so many other outlaws he had met, hemmed in by rules until they could not live. He sat there with his bottle, but no longer drinking, only thoughtful; now he was alone in the room, save for the bartender, a huge man with a slack, stupid face.

From the room behind the bar, a woman's voice suddenly shrieked in fear and horror. "No. Please, no!"

Fargo heard, as it tailed out, a bubblous laugh.

He'd found what he'd come here for; now it was time to leave, and there would never be a better chance. But not without his shotgun. And Garfield was obviously very busy. Fargo picked up the bottle, went to the bar. "I'd like a fresh glass," he said.

The slack-faced giant only stared at him. Fargo said, "Dammit, a fresh glass." The man frowned, turned uncertainly toward the shelves behind him. Fargo swung the bottle.

It made a sound like a melon falling off a wagon as it connected. The big man sighed, fell behind the bar. Fargo grinned, pleased he'd got his twenty dollars worth. He drew the Colt, went to the door. The thing about a place like this, he mused, was that it all hung on one man's reputation and one man's shotgun. Dogan's rep, and maybe Garfield's, had everybody buffaloed, and Garfield, anyhow, in his lust, had grown slack. Fargo stepped back a pace, sizing up the door, then threw his hard body against it with all his strength.

A wooden latch screamed, gave. The door slammed open, Fargo lurched into a small, foul-smelling room. Garfield turned from the bed in one corner, his huge belly spilling over pants he was just about to shuck. The girl on the bed lay drawn up in a tight knot, back to Fargo, and he could tell nothing about her. Garfield blinked, then his big body moved with amazing speed as he reached for Fargo's shotgun on the table.

Fargo fired two rounds from the Colt, straight into Garfield's belly. Exploding, those hollow-points, in flesh, they drove Garfield back before his hand touched the Fox. The room was sprayed with bits of him, and yet his thickness was such that neither slug had reached a vital place. He squealed, and his hand dug for his Colt, and Fargo raised his aim. The third bullet left almost nothing of Garfield's thicklipped face. It was like a mountain falling when that gross bulk hit the floor. Fargo spun, reaching for the shotgun. At the same instant, the girl rolled over, staring.

Fargo snatched up the Fox, trained it on her. "Don't yell," he said.

"Thank God," she said. "You killed him." She was young, not far into her twenties, long-legged, slim-bellied and lean hipped, with small, pointed breasts. Her face, framed by tangled blonde hair, was striking, blue eyes, short nose, red mouth, firm chin. "He's dead!" she cried out with growing triumph.

Fargo had no time to waste, but she was worth a look. "You're Dogan's daughter." Then it hit him: a hostage. "Up," he rasped. "Find some clothes, git 'em on, and hurry. You're comin' with me."

Longlashed eyes blinked. "I don't understand, but—away from here? Yes. Oh, God, yes!" She sprang off the bed, and Fargo whirled to face the door, in case the shots had drawn anybody. But, as he'd expected, all the guards were on the outer edges of Brown's Hole, looking for people coming in, not those going out. Over-confident, he thought. Run a place too long your own way and you get the big head.

Now the girl had on a shirt and Levis. She reached for boots, but Fargo seized her arm. "Come on. You move ahead. You're Dogan's daughter, and anybody comes at me, you get it."

He did not expect the surprising strength with which she wrenched away. "I'm not his daughter. My name's Sara Raven! I'll never take his name." She put out a hand, seized his arm. "If you're leaving, I'll come with you, anywhere, but . . . don't you understand? I'm not his daughter!"

"Way I understand it, you'll do 'til one comes along. Move!"

She looked at him, eyes, blazing, then said "Yeah, I'll move." Back straight, she strode ahead of him, out of the room. Fargo saw the musette bag that held his extra ammo, slipped it over one arm, followed.

The outer bar room was deserted, the bartender still unconscious from that full-powered bottle blow. Sara Raven's head swiveled as she surveyed it. Then she said, "Horses! Out the back!"

"What?"

"That's where the horses are!" She was already running toward the back door, nimble as an antelope. Fargo hesitated, followed.

It opened to a yard, and on the other side of that was a corral. Two saddled horses drowsed at its rails, both superb animals. Sara blurted: "Garfield always kept them here, his get-away mounts." She unlatched reins, swung up. Fargo was right behind her. Somehow, in this moment, leadership had passed to her.

Sara swung her horse around, and for a moment her eyes met his. "I don't know who you are," she snapped, "but you're a long cry from Garfield or Dogan. I'm past caring. I'll help you get out of here and you can have the rest of it, too, but for God's sake, if you're running, stick by me and help me get away, too!"

Fargo understood, then: understood the desperation of this lean, lovely girl sold by a killer stepfather to a gross monstrosity like Garfield. "I'm with you," he rasped. "Don't worry." His hands caressed the shotgun, and its cold-steel feel, almost part of his own flesh, told him everything was all right. He raised the weapon with a wild exultancy, two spare rounds from the musette bag in his hand. "Ride. Head south, downriver, and take us out of this."

Her answer was, "Hiiyaah!" She kicked the horse, leaned forward in the saddle, long legs gripping, body balanced, a fine rider. The animal rocketed around the store building, and Fargo's was right behind. As they came into the clear, his overtook and he was in the lead. He saw four men pour out of a cabin, gaping. One reached for a gun, and the other stayed his hand. They were the horse-thieves.

"Ride out, Sara!" one yelled, and it was obvious they knew her and were on her side. Sara didn't answer, only lashed the horse with reins and bent into the wind and headed through the scattering of huts, bearing on a course that led downriver, long blonde hair streaming out behind.

But it was not to be that easy. The last hut on the outskirts disgorged three men, in time to see Fargo and Sara racing toward them. Fargo heard a shout borne on the wind's whip: "That's Garfield's girl and she's runnin'! Stop her, or Dogan'll have our hides!" They scattered, drawing sixguns. Fargo lashed the mount, made a length ahead of Sara. On his left, he saw a bearded man on one knee, arm outstretched, Colt in hand, other hand locking wrist as he tracked Sara. Fargo fired the right barrel, pointing the shotgun across his body.

It bucked, roared, and the man screamed, went backwards. Fargo turned in the saddle, saw the other two, side by side, staring, guns upraised. No time to inquire their intentions: he loosed nine buckshot on the run from the left barrel.

They spread, those lethal pellets, in a wide, terrible screen. Both men screamed as they were caught simultaneously by the blast. Then they went down, kicking. It did not matter to Fargo whether they were dead or not, as long as they were out of action. He broke the shotgun, thrust in two fresh rounds, and Sara, eyes wide, awed, came up alongside.

"Who *are* you?" she screamed.

"Fargo!" he yelled back, and spurred the horse.

Now they were racing through the meadows, heading for the cover of the cottonwoods. Forty miles, Fargo thought. Damned near that much before they made the boats, a full day's travel and possibly fighting all the way. As if to confirm his foreboding, he heard hoofbeats coming from the right, saw Lew and Billy, drawn from their guard-posts at the ferry by the sound of gunfire, pounding toward him, rifles raised. A bullet slapped by his head as they opened fire, out of shotgun range.

"Keep low!" Fargo bawled. "Head for those woods!"

Sara heard him, sank in her saddle, sheltered by the horse's neck. Fargo slipped forward like an Indian, heel hooked over the saddle, arm around his mount's neck, other hand free to fire beneath it. Their fine horses pounded toward the cottonwoods, two hundred yards away. Lew and Billy chased, shooting as they came. Dogan men, he thought, those two, through and through.

Just for the hell of it, he fired both barrels under the horse's neck. At that range, the pattern spread until only one pellet struck. Billy's mount, stung by it, sheered off, bucked. Lew hesitated. That gave Sara time to gain the woods, and Fargo thundered into underbrush right behind her. "Take cover!" he bawled, checked his mount, swung down into thick headhigh greenery, sprouts and vines, and rammed two more shells from the musette bag into the gun.

Through the tracery pattern of the brush he saw them coming, Billy, mount under control, Lew pounding ahead. Sara had dismounted behind him in the woods. Fargo waited. The two rounds should be enough, but he had to stand up to rifle fire until the range was right.

Rifle fire: they pumped it at him. It whined and slapped all around his head, from two Winchesters, clipping twigs and leaves. He judged he had time, took out a cigar, lit it quickly, drew in smoke. With it clamped between his teeth, he waited as they thundered down on him. If they stayed together, that would make it easy.

They didn't, Lew bawling something, sheering off. He was in the lead, and as he went out to the right, Fargo took him first, lining the shotgun, judging range, and when Lew was a yard inside the effective reach, firing the right barrel.

The big spread of double-zero buckshot made a wall. Lew and the horse both ran into it, and both went down. Fargo saw its damage, regretted what it did to the horse, but there was no help. Anyhow, it killed mount and rider simultaneously. The horse collapsed, and Lew went rolling and never got up again; and Billy saw that and pulled up and Fargo pivoted and fired the left barrel.

Billy's horse screamed, went over backwards, fell on him. Then it scrambled up. Something flopped obscenely on its back: the body of a man, punched and anchored by the saddle horn that had gone straight through his body. As the horse stampeded, Billy bounced on its back, and he was not quite dead, he made a thin, keening sound. Fargo spun away, reloaded the shotgun, put foot in stirrup, swung up. "Ride out, Sara," he yelled, saw her swing up and spurred his mount.

They made two miles through the cottonwoods, entered a thicket of sprouts and willows shaded by immense trees, rubbled with driftwood from high water. Fargo gave the command to draw up.

She reined in, spun her horse, face pale, huge eyes staring. "Stranger, who are you?"

"Fargo," he rasped. "I told you that."

It took a moment, and then she whispered, "That Fargo?"

"You've heard of me?"

"Dogan has. He's talked about looking for you."

"Looking for me?"

"He's a shotgun man, they say you are. God knows, I believe it now. You're as good as Dogan, maybe better."

"Listen," Fargo said, "we'll talk about that later. Right now we've got to make it to the end of Brown's Hole and meet up with some people. You know this country and you know where the guards are?"

"Do I? I've never been any place else. Only here and Cord's Park and the river—"

Fargo felt as if a cold wind played over him. "Cord's Park?"

"A valley down by the Crossing of the Fathers. A man named Tom Cord was there when Dogan came. They threw in together and—"

"I see," Fargo murmured. "Yeah, I see." He glanced around to make sure there was no immediate pursuit. "Sara." His hand closed on her wrist. "You want to get away from here?"

"I told you, I've got to." Her voice was desperate. "You think I want to wind up a plaything for . . . for men like Garfield? You came just in time. I'd managed to fight him off so far, but—" She shook her head. "Fargo, I don't know you, but please trust me, you've got to trust me—"

"I trust you," Fargo said, the whole thing clear now. "But you're gonna have to trust me. I want some answers. You ever hear of a man named Knight?"

"You mean Colonel Knight, the engineer?"

"He's the one," Fargo said quickly, pulses pounding.

"Of course. Dogan's got him, in Cord's Park. Knight and four others."

"Ahh," Fargo said. "So they didn't drown."

"Drown? Some of them did, going through Cataract Canyon. But they'd already been spotted, anyhow. Cord went out to meet them, Dogan sent him. He posed as a trapper, claimed to be able to guide them. He led them right into Cord's Park, down below Dandy Crossing, what they call Hite's Ferry. The ferry's in Dogan's hands and so's the Park and —Dogan's men and Cord killed a lot of them. But five of them were left alive. Dogan—I won't call him anything else, he's not my father, he's not! He's not even my stepfather, he never married my mother, just took her!— Dogan took 'em and has kept 'em ever since, in case lawmen ever come down in here and he needs something to buy his way out. He keeps them locked up, treated like dogs, but they're still alive and—"

"That's all I need to know," Fargo said, voice ringing like stroke of hammer on an anvil. "Mount up, woman, and take me out of here. You lead and I'll do the fighting. I've got boats waiting at the end of Brown's Hole, and if you play ball with me, those boats will take you outside and I'll see you're set up good in a big town and properly looked after."

Sara's eyes seemed to glow. "What town? A town as big as Yuma?"

"Let's talk about Oyster Bay, Long Island," Fargo said. "And New York City. But later. For now, let's ride."

* * *

They took it more slowly now. Sara said that Garfield had guards posted all along both sides of the river, in order to give alarm if any substantial party passed through. "There's two things Dogan was scared of," she told Fargo. "First was maybe a big expedition of lawmen. Second was any kind of outfit that might open up this country. When he saw those Knight people using all those fancy instruments, he knew he had to take them . . ."

They worked their way along the floodplain, keeping to the cottonwoods, and, with Sara's expert knowledge, dodging guards. By nightfall, they were far down Brown's Hole. Fargo only rested the horses, made no fire, cooked no meal. When their mounts were ready, they rode again. This time through the humid darkness and swampy traps of the Green's tidewater; but Sara Raven knew every foot of the way. She never led Fargo false, and even in the moonless fastness of the woods they made good time.

Daylight was not far off when Sara finally reined in. "Fargo, it's not more than a mile or two to the end of where you can take a horse downriver." She swayed in the saddle with fatigue, but she had guts, was a stayer. "If you've got an outfit waitin', they're bound to be in the mudflats below what we call Double Buttes."

104

"Maybe," Fargo said. He had not told her that the boats he was trying to reach were guided by Tom Cord. If the boats weren't there . . . well, that was something he did not want to think about. Because if Cord had somehow moved them, talked Vane into going on down-river. . . . Like baby mice in a bottle, Fargo thought. That's how we'll be in Brown's Hole. No way to get out, none at all . . .

He remembered his final conference with Cord and Vane. Twin Buttes, they'd been called on the map. "The boats are supposed to be there," he said. "Lead on."

They threaded their way through swampy bottomlands, heavily wooded with cottonwoods and willows and a few stray aspens, ever closer to the river's edge. Then Sara struck a trail. "This ought to take us to the last place any boats can be, under Double Buttes."

They followed it in the gray light of false dawn. Now Fargo could hear the familiar river's rush, muted here, yet still strong. "I'll go in front," he said and tilted the shotgun out across the saddle. The horse edged through dim, fog-shrouded woods at a walking gait with Sara close behind. Fargo was completely tense, all his concentration focused, ready to fight or run. The boats could be there, the boats could be gone, or there could be an ambush in their place.

Horses' hooves made squelching sounds in the mud. Now the river was only a few dozen yards away. Out of the fog, a dim figure reared. "Who goes there?" it demanded, and Fargo saw the muzzle of a rifle trained on him, and despite that, the tension slacked.

"Michaelson," he said, "It's Fargo."

The young engineer stepped out of the willows, stared at Fargo, grinned. Then, when he looked at Sara Raven, his grin went away. "Fargo—"

"Explain it later. Everybody there where they're supposed to be?"

"Of course. We had some trouble with Cord; he wanted to move the outfit past where you said to stay. But Vane and I talked him down. Fargo, this young lady . . ."

"Mr. Michaelson, meet Miss Raven. She and I have run off from Brown's Hole together. I'll put her in your charge." Fargo swayed slightly in the saddle with weariness, but he mastered that feeling. There was much, he thought, that he still had to do. "Take us down to camp, Michaelson," he said.

Chapter VI

The boats had been efficiently hidden in reeds and willows: it was, according to Fargo's instructions, a fireless camp that had been made higher in the cottonwoods. Daylight had just begun to fall into it as he rode in, with Michaelson and Sara following at a much slower pace, the engineer walking at her horse's head. When Fargo saw the gray forms of the tents, he swung down, and at once Vane was hustling up the path to meet him, with Cord right behind him.

"Fargo! Damn, man, it's good to see you back! Did you learn anything?"

Fargo didn't meet Vane's outstretched hand and his gaze went past the Captain to Cord. "Well, I learned considerable," he said, and he lined the shotgun. "One of the things I learned is that Cord's a goddam spy. He's the one betrayed Knight to the outlaws."

"Fargo—?" Vane began, but Fargo shoved him aside. He confronted the bulky Cord now, the shotgun aimed. "Leave me alone, Vane," he said. "I've got things to settle. Cord, you're Dogan's man."

"I never heard of Dogan," Cord growled, but his face was taut.

"Sara Raven says you did."

"Sara—" Cord's eyes lifted. He saw Michaelson coming, the girl's weary figure on the horse. His jaw dropped. Then his gaze went to the shotgun and in the dawn light his face was like something cast from tallow. "Now, wait—"

"No waiting," Fargo said. "The Colonel trusted you and you pulled a double-cross. Part of Dogan's operation's to have spies everywhere. You were on hand in Yuma, weren't you, when the Colonel came looking for a guide—?"

"Fargo," Cord began. Then his mouth twitched, his hand flashed for his gun. Two things happened simultaneously. Fargo fired both barrels of the Fox, and Vane struck it down, and all eighteen buckshot plowed into the mud. And Yadkin, the geologist, seized Cord's wrist with both strong hands and twisted and Cord's Colt fell free. As it landed in the mud, Cord whirled, smashed a fist into Yadkin's face. The man fell back, and Cord began to run, heading for the boats.

Vane was still holding the shotgun; Fargo released it. He dashed through a screen of willow sprouts after Cord, fishing Colt from holster. Now, in the gray light, he made out the boats in an inlet.

Cord leaped into the hinter one, cast off, seized a paddle, shoved. The boat stuck in the mud. Fargo came up alongside. "Cord!" he bellowed, and Cord swung the paddle. It hit the barrel of the Colt and ripped the gun from Fargo's hand. Cord laughed, and the boat backed, headed for midstream. Fargo reached for the gun, saw it covered, its barrel plugged with muck. As Cord, in the stern, backed the boat, Fargo sprang into the prow.

Cord gave a mighty shove, the craft moved out into the current. Then Cord threw the paddle amidships and his hand flashed behind him. When it came up, the fourteen-inch blade of Cord's Bowie glinted in the sunrise.

Cord balanced on limber legs, knife thrust out before him. Yellow teeth shone under peeled back lips as he said, "All right, Big Ugly. Game's played my way now." The boat swung into the current, moved downstream.

"We'll check that," Fargo said, and his own knees caught the rhythm of the moving craft, and then Cord came at him, lunging straight down the boat, knife out. Fargo's hand flashed back of his empty holster to where the Batangas knife was sheathed. It came out, he flipped his wrist, the buffalo-horn handles flipped and locked and the ten inch blade was naked. He brought it up just in time to make it chime against and deflect Cord's knife as the boat picked up speed, sliding swiftly down the river. Fargo's wrist-strength and the tempered blade made Cord's Bowie sheer away, and then Fargo went for Cord's gut, but Cord blocked him with the blade.

109

They knew each other now and both fell back a pace, and the boat went on, bucking. Cord dropped into a crouch, and Fargo followed suit, blade of the Batangas knife parallel to the ground in his right hand, chin down, gut sucked in, arm across it, and then they came at one another. Steel rang on steel, and Cord tried to hack his way past Fargo's guard, and the Bowie had this advantage which the Batangas knife lacked: a big wrist-guard. Fargo's blade deflected Cord's attack, bound straight for entrails, but Cord's blade leaped up, slid over the small guard of the Filipino knife and laid open the back of Fargo's wrist. Fargo felt no pain, but he yielded. Cord came in again, and both men had injured rights, now; Fargo's newly cut and Cord's where Fargo's teeth had bitten. That was irony: bandages protected the inside of Cord's wrist, where the blood was.

Thrust and parry, ring of knife on knife and the boat bucking under them, rushing on. Fargo, pinned against the bow compartment, dared not turn his head to see what the boom of water behind him meant; Cord bore in, blade a winking flicker in the rays of sunlight falling down into the river bed.

"You're a shotgun man!" Cord rasped. "But cold steel's my weapon! I'll skin you the way I've skinned a lot of critters!" And he came in again, knife darting forward like a snake's tongue.

Fargo caught it on his own blade, tried to lift. Cord's weight and strength were too much. Cord's blade came loose and ripped toward Fargo's belly. Fargo twisted and felt the cool whisk of steel go past, and in that instant he took his gamble. He flipped the knife from injured right to left, caught it deftly and then Cord's flank was wholly open. Fargo aimed the blade and fell forward, and even as Cord drew back for another stroke, he felt the tempered steel go through flesh, glance off bone, go in deeper, and he twisted it and ripped downward.

Cord screamed as entrails bulged through the wound. He turned, raised the knife, cramped at his belly with his left hand. Fargo slashed Cord's wrist, bandage and all and the knife fell away and Cord reeled back, eyes wide, as Fargo came in again, going up and in, hard, on the left side of Cord's breastbone, aiming for the heart.

He felt the small guard of the Batangas knife collide with flesh. He turned the blade, withdrew. Cord sat down hard on the rushing boat's center thwart. He stared at Fargo. He rose. Then he whirled, and as his legs gave way, he fell overboard into the river.

The tan water swallowed him as if it could devour a million like him before its appetite was sated. Fargo caught a glimpse of a slack face trailing blood from its mouth before it plunged under. Then he staggered backwards, sat down hard on the bow compartment. He held the knife in the river, washed its blade. There wasn't much in his stomach, but he tossed what there was into the Green, rackingly. And then he lifted his head and heard the rapids' roar.

Turning, he saw the rocks like teeth in a shark's jaw arrayed before him. Vaguely, he knew there was something he must do. A sandbar lay on the right side of the river, and it seemed to him he had to make that. But a paddle wouldn't do it, would be like a fly swatter in an invasion of locusts. He lurched to the center thwart, unshipped the oars, dropped them into locks. He leaned back, sinking them into water.

Just in time, he braked the boat. Water sucked and gurgled at the blades, as he leaned all his weight, summoned all his strength, into the bite of the right oar.

It was enough, but just barely. The boat turned in the current, rushed to the left bank. Fargo heard sand grate as it grounded, just short of the rocks. He summoned strength to leap out, drag the boat up higher. Then he sat down on the sandbar, exhausted from two days of action without sleep, and waited for the others to join him.

Presently they did, the whole outfit rushing down the stream and Sara Raven, with yellow hair flying out behind, just behind Michaelson in the second boat.

* * *

The camp was well hidden in a cleft in the canyon walls, after a twenty-mile run down the Green. In the darkness, the river made its continual seething rush, and occasionally there was the splash of rock falling from the canyon walls above the mainstream. Flickering firelight cast a yellow pattern on the face of the girl, weary and still full of shock, and on the faces of the men around her.

"So there it is." Fargo said harshly, bone weary himself. "Double-Barrel Dogan's still alive, and he's down there somewhere—" he gestured toward the south. "And he has Colonel Knight and four men penned up like hogs, waiting to be slaughtered if anybody comes against him. Cord's Park, below the Crossing of the Fathers, just above the Arizona line. Full of outlaws, Sara says; thirty, forty, of the old wild crew holed up there. Well, there ain't no help for it. We got to go in there somehow and get Knight out."

Vane paced back and forth restlessly. "Fargo, I don't see how we can do it. The girl says that place is a fortress, locked in by canyons all around. Only one entrance, and that fortified. How can nine men go up against such odds?"

"I've faced longer ones," Fargo said. "Besides, what else could we do?"

"Leave the river. Get word to the Colonel. Then have the Utah state authorities move. Send in a huge posse, or the Army . . ."

Fargo tipped back the cavalry hat, looked at Vane wryly. "You served under Colonel Knight. You got a grudge against him?"

"Grudge? Of course not! He's one of the finest men I ever knew."

"Well, you talk like you want to see him dead," Fargo said harshly. "Send a bunch of troops blundering in there, Dogan'll know they're coming days before they get there and be long gone. And he won't take Knight with him. He'll do like Garfield said they did with spies. Kill him, slit his body open, stuff it full of rocks and roll him in the river. No, there ain't but one way to do it. And that's for

113

the nine of us to tackle Cord's Park ourselves and get Knight out, somehow."

"And I say it's impossible! First of all, we've got the whole state of Utah to cross! A third of the Colorado River, and the worst third at that, to run! And we no longer even have a guide—"

"Better none than Cord," Fargo said. "He'd have guided us, all right—straight into a trap."

"Just the same—"

"Captain Vane." The girl's voice was quiet, but there was a firmness in it that cut through Vane's words, made them all turn and look.

Sara Raven got to her feet and, tired as she was, wet and dirty as her clothing was, she was something to see, Fargo told himself, a lot of woman. Her next words confirmed that. "I can guide you," she said.

Vane stared. "You?"

"I grew up down here, remember? I've never really been anywhere else. And . . . I've told you how Dogan operated. Two main hideouts—Brown's Hole in the north, Cord's Park in the south. Dogan travels two, three times a year between them. Rides the back country upstream, shoots the river down. I've made the trip a lot of times. I'm sure I can show you the way."

Vane frowned. "Young lady, I'm not certain—"

"And Fargo's right. He'll kill Colonel Knight and all the rest if he thinks he has to run. You send in the Army, they're as good as dead. But I know everything about Cord's Park, where he keeps the guards, all of it. Maybe, just maybe, you men could get in there and get Knight's crew out, if I showed you how."

"That's an offer we'll take," Fargo said promptly.

"You hold on. Miss Raven—"

"I tell you," she said, and her eyes glowed in the firelight, "you can do it if I help you. And I will help you on one condition." She turned to Fargo. "I want Dogan dead."

There was silence. "Dogan!" she broke it at last, bitterly. "He killed my real father, destroyed my mother, gave me to that swine Garfield ... If Fargo hadn't come when he did, I'd already decided: I was going to get a gun, kill Garfield and myself." She drew in a breath that made breasts rise beneath the wet shirt. "But it's Dogan I really want. He's an . . . an animal, a killer animal, and he doesn't deserve to live. I'll do anything to see him dead! And if you'll help me, I'll guide you down the river and into Cord's Park!"

Vane stared at her a moment, then turned to Fargo. "You think there's no other way?"

"I know there ain't," said Fargo.

"Then I guess we're in for it. Very well, Miss Raven, we accept your offer. But—" He grinned without any humor as he looked at Fargo. "As you know, I have no combat experience."

"That's all right; I got enough for both of us."

"What I mean to say is this. I can't guarantee how much help I'll be in a fight, since I've never been tested under fire. But with Miss Raven's help, I'll get this outfit to Cord's Park somehow—and then we'll see how I react when the bullets fly."

This was a man talking, and Fargo smiled. "I

ain't worried about that." He stood up. "Then it's settled. All right, post a guard. Michaelson, you and Birdsong take first watch. Yadkin and Randall get the second. Sara, you can have my blankets and I'll take Cord's. He claimed to be a trapper, and, God knows, he smelled like one. And . . . the rest of it." He stroked his shotgun. "That part about Dogan . . ." Despite his weariness, he felt that almost sick eagerness. "When we reach Cord's Park, I'll see to that . . ."

Lodore Canyon lay ahead of them; by first daylight they were up, camp struck, boats loaded. Sara's face was grave. "It's a good twenty miles," she said, "and some of the roughest water on the river. Two falls, they call 'em Upper and Lower Disaster. But I'm pretty sure I know the way all right."

"Nothing to do but try," Fargo said. "Let's move out."

She settled in the bow of the lead boat, picked up a paddle, and he saw at once she could use it as well as any man in the crew. What she lacked in strength, she made up in skill, and she was cool, deft, as they pushed up and the current took them.

Cord had been right: what had gone before was child's play. But Lodore was deadly serious. Here the river split straight through a mountain so that walls thousands of feet in height loomed above them, shutting out the sunlight. And, so Powell's early measurement had showed, it dropped over four hundred feet from end to end of canyon, most of that in a twelve-mile space.

First a few small rapids, like the bait in a trap. Then the rush was faster, water whiter, boiling, spuming. And now the boats were runaway stallions again, racing, bucking, and after that it was as if they were birds, and flying. Fargo worked desperately with paddle and with the oars; Sara made split-second decisions, always right, pointing out the course. They ran gantlet after gantlet of hungry rocks, fought the sucking, whirling current, taking longer risks every second. They leaped through the narrow channel of Upper Disaster Falls, rocketed on past an island, swirled on down. Then Lower Disaster loomed ahead, and well-named. Here the canyon wall turned right angles to the stream, and the Green had cut right through it. They entered a kind of tunnel, with the wall hanging over them, fought to keep from being thrown against the side. Then Fargo sucked in his breath. The tunnel was three-sided: the water-carved ceiling hanging over them, the canyon wall on their flank, the fierce river's surface. And ahead the ceiling lowered, and where the current rushed beneath it, the clearance was less than two feet high. Three minutes, two, and they'd be slammed hard into that closing pinch of rock—.

Sara gave a signal, dug in with her paddle. Fargo got a bite with the right oar. At the last second, just before it seemed inevitable that boat and all its occupants must smash full into the rock, the craft's prow swung out. The current split here, and Sara had caught the outside swirl, and now the boat raced toward midstream once more. Fargo twisted, saw Vane, with superb skill, make the transition in exactly the same spot, and Randall, the Coast Guardsman, follow just as deftly. Sara turned, too, for one brief instant: Fargo saw eyes shining, face glowing with excitement. Far from being frightened, she was exhilarated, jubilant. She laughed, the sound swallowed by the water, and Fargo grinned, and then, once again, they fought the river.

Yet all this was only preliminary. Ahead lay the stretch called Hell's Half Mile. Fargo hardly saw it; when the boats raced into its foaming, boiling downward slide, there was no longer vision, only flashes, disconnected impressions like the fragments of a dream. Now they raced faster than the fastest horse could run, at express train speed, through spray and fume. A rock here on the right, fend it off; a slab of boulder there, dead ahead: the boat sheered around it. A fall, a leap into the air, plunge into water, and yet the craft shook itself, shot on. Never even in his logging days had he made such a ride, never worked so fast, so desperately, to keep afloat, never faced such risks. And then, somehow, the lead boat was through, and as the water slacked a little, Sara swung it toward a sandbar. Fargo turned once more, as Birdsong, behind him, cried out, and then he swore. Vane's boat, leaping through the rapids just behind them swung suddenly too far right. It struck a rock, turned broadside, went over. Suddenly Vane, just as Fargo's boat grounded on the bar, disappeared into the river. The other two of his crew caught the overturned boat, hung on, but Vane was swallowed by the spuming current.

"Birdsong!" Fargo yelled. "Hold up here and watch my gear!" He rammed the shotgun in Birdsong's hand, shrugged out of bandoliers, threw off his hat. "Fargo!" Sara screamed, but he was already in the river.

Here, he had already seen, it shallowed, had heard the boat grate on rocks. His booted feet found bottom, he braced himself against the furious current. Fighting it, he half-swam, half-waded into the channel. Now it was around his chest, sucking at him, trying to drag him under. He fought against its mighty strength with all his own, and then he saw the bobbing figure, Vane, struggling feebly, already full of water, head breaking surface, disappearing.

And now it was a deadly race. The river threatened to take Vane's body out past Fargo's right by five yards or ten. He had to close that gap. Vaguely, he was aware that his own boat was putting out, Birdsong at the oars. He turned sideways to the current, waded on, still chest deep. Three yards, he made, four, and then his feet went out from under him. He was slammed into a rock, went under, caught his balance, came up spitting water. Vane's body was like a cork, only a few yards away, and now Vane was no longer struggling. Fargo made a desperate lunge.

It was just enough: his fingers hooked in the captain's belt. Then both men were carried down the stream. Over and over they rolled, Vane dead weight, Fargo's strength unable to control their progress. His feet sought bottom, touched it, were swept away again. Still, he never slacked his grip on Vane.

And now there was no more bottom and they were both in the current and this could be the end. Fargo gasped for air as his head went under, came up, and he fought with powerful strokes of his left arm and kicking legs to right himself. But Vane dragged him down and there was no chance to get a carry. Either he let the captain go or he died himself . . .

Then, through the roar of water, he heard the woman's voice, its shrillness carrying. "Fargo! Here!" He went under, surfaced, shook water from his eyes and saw it, Sara in the prow, holding out a paddle, as Birdsong fought with oars to maneuver the boat and hold it stable. Fargo made a frantic grasp, missed, and Sara screamed and swung the paddle, and this time his left hand seized the blade and he hung on. Birdsong yelled something, dug in with the oars, and the boat turned around, dragging Vane and Fargo with it as Sara braced herself, and now everything depended on the girl's strength.

River-bred, she had plenty of it. Somehow she managed the weight of two men with the river sucking at them, as Birdsong put into shore. Fargo found bottom, dug in his feet; then, gasping, exhausted, he struggled out on a sandbar, dragging Vane with him. The second boat came tumbling down the river, lodged against a rock, two men clinging to it. Fargo, spreading Vane out on the sand face down, spitting water himself through mouth and nostrils, saw Sara put the boat into the stream again.

He turned his attention to the captain. Van lay still, but his chest rose and fell with breathing. Fargo drained water from him, after checking Vane's mouth with two fingers and straightening out his swallowed tongue. He saw a purple bruise, a swelling knot, on Vane's skull just behind the eye, where Vane had hit a rock. Then Sara's boat was coming in with the other in tow, and the third craft, coming unscathed through the rapids, followed.

Birdsong leaped out. "Fargo, you all right?"

"Whiskey," Fargo gasped. "A bottle in the back compartment."

Birdsong went after it. Sara dropped to her knees beside him. "Neal, oh, Neal. You almost drowned."

"Almost don't count," Fargo whispered. He turned his head, looked at her through blurry eyes, and what he saw in hers was almost as good as the whiskey, when Birdsong came with it.

But there was Vane to see to first. Fargo poured a drink down Vane's throat, had one himself, passed the bottle to Michaelson and the corporal in Vane's crew. By the time it came back to him, Vane groaned, stirred, and Fargo helped him sit up and gave him another drink.

"Judas," Vane whispered. "Close, damned close."

"We'll make camp here," Fargo said. "Randall, check the boats. See what we lost in that turnover and report."

"I know we lost our rifles," Michaelson said.

Fargo's heart sank. A fight in the offing and three

long guns gone. "Well, it can't be helped. Anyhow, you saved your pistols. We'll see about more rifles later."

"See about—?" Michaelson blinked. "From where?"

"I don't know. Take 'em off of Dogan's men, I guess. Let's get under cover in those willows."

*　*　*

Vane was tough. By nightfall, with some coffee in him and some food, he was his usual brisk, efficient self. He, Fargo, Michaelson, Yadkin, Randall and Sara sat around a fire, map spread out. "We should have lined those last rapids," Fargo said.

"No." Vane's voice was crisp. "It was my fault. Spray blinded me, and I missed a turn Miss Raven made. I'll not let that happen again . . ."

"All the same," Fargo said, "it's too long a chance. We can't lose more guns."

"Then disassemble and stow your guns," Sara cut in. "You won't need them anyhow between here and the Dandy Crossing. From now on, it's mostly white water. We'll be going so fast and the cliffs are so high that nobody could hit us. And . . . if you're going to save Colonel Knight, you'd better not waste any time. There'll be boats behind us and riders circling the back country to carry the word about Garfield to Dogan. We've got to outrun 'em. The river's the fastest way to do that, but not if you take time to line the boats." Her voice was suddenly intense. "Believe me, I know the way. If you'll only follow exactly—"

122

"We will," Vane said. "You've certainly proved yourself as guide today." He turned to Fargo. "This is in my area of authority. We'll not line the boats. We'll make the fastest possible time to Cord's Park."

Fargo looked at him and grinned. "Vane, don't ever worry about your guts. You've got more of 'em than one man needs." He finished mopping the shotgun with oil, worked its action, crammed in two fresh, dry shells. "Now, I'm gonna take a look around."

He scouted the willows, found nothing to alarm him. He was just turning back toward camp when he brought the shotgun up, lined it. "Who's there?" he rasped.

"Don't shoot, it's me," said Sara Raven softly. She came through the screen of brush, a dim figure in the moonlight. "The others have already turned in. I couldn't rest . . ."

Fargo lowered the sawed-off Fox. "What's wrong?"

"I don't know. I just . . . never felt like this before. It's the first time in so many years I've been free of Dogan . . . the first time I've been with men who weren't Dogan's kind, long riders." She hesitated. "Fargo, you said you'd take me to a city."

"I said that, yes. If I come out of this, I will. I always keep my promises."

"I thought you would. It's part of what you are." She moved closer to him. "I have so much to thank you for . . . few minutes more back there in Brown's Hole and Garfield would have . . . I don't think I could have lived with myself then."

Fargo cradled the shotgun in his arm. "He hadn't, when I killed him?"

"No. I had just been . . . delivered to him before you got there. I fought him and he knocked me around, and then you came . . ." She took his hand. "I don't mean that I am . . . you know. There was a boy I thought, when I was younger, that I loved. But Dogan killed him . . ."

"I'm sorry," Fargo said.

"The past is past. I'll live for the future now." Her face, caught by a ray of moonlight, was very white, her hair combed down around it, glinting, her eyes enormous, her lips parted. "Neal . . ."

"Yes," Fargo said, and he bent and kissed her.

She came against him desperately, arms encircling him.

They were like that for a long time, locked together, her body moving subtly against his. After a while, she wrenched away. "Neal," she whispered again.

"Yes," Fargo repeated. He laid the shotgun aside. As she began to unbutton her shirt, there on the grassy flat in the willows, a huge rock fell from the rim into the river. But they did that all the time and he ignored it, as she sank down on the grass and he went to her.

Chapter VII

They raced downriver, through white water and sometimes calm, often at express train speed, occasionally rowing and paddling where the current slackened. Sometimes they had to line the boats, hard, dangerous work; sometimes they portaged, which was even harder. But only as a last resort; for they knew their race was against time. "All this back country," Sara told them, "is full of long riders hiding out. Both sides of the river, from Brown's Hole to Cord's Park, wherever there aren't any settlements. But Dogan supplies and rules them all, and when he gets words that Garfield's dead and I've run away, he'll have these canyon rims crawling with them. We've got to make it to Cord's Park before riders can cross-country. Or we won't make it at all."

So they ran on, never slowing, setting, so Vane claimed, a new run for the navigation of the Colorado.

Past the Yampa's mouth and Echo Cliffs; through the mad race of Whirlpool Canyon and the magnificence of Rainbow Park: Split Mountain Gorge and Desolation Canyon: deserted gold dredges and a ghost town; past lonesome ranches and past the junction of the Grand, which, with the Green, formed the Colorado proper. Through Cataract Canyon and past the old Dandy Crossing of the Robbers' Roost bunch. And they faced dangers and encountered marvels that none of them, not even Fargo, had dreamed of before. Rapids, falls, whirlpools, always those, and sometimes a boat would capsize, but by good luck they lost no men and no equipment of importance. Or one would splinter on a rock, but Randall always managed a quick, deft repair . . . But the water was not the only threat: there were the canyon walls themselves, from which ancient boulders that had held their grip for centuries suddenly let go and fell at random, like great missiles hurled by playful, careless gods. There was never any knowing when one might crash squarely on a boat; near-misses were far too plentiful.

Worse were the landslides, when a whole segment of canyon wall gave way and rushed thousands of feet down a slope into the river. Wherever that massive bulk of dirt and rock hit—and one nearly engulfed them, would have, if Fargo had not heard its growl just in time and seen its terrible movement ahead of them—it changed the navigation of the river, altering channels, creating brand new rapids.

Thunderstorms were frequent, too, and, with lightning playing back and forth between cliffs a thousand feet in height, whole storms were trapped inside the gorge—no human could not be terrified by the fire and tremendous echoing thunder. High water followed, floods rushing downstream and carrying their boats like chips. Even Fargo was awed by the magnitude of the great gash the river had carved in earth: here was nothing he could fight with guns or fists; this was the Colorado, and it gave not a damn for the nine ant-like creatures on its roaring surface, trapped within its walls.

But often it rewarded their bravery with splendor: breathtaking bursts of color as sun struck the striated, mineral-filled cliffs about them; whole lost cities and forgotten palaces of windcarved rock that glowed like jewels, and real cities, too, lost and abandoned: ancient cliff dwellings, vast mud towns clinging high up on the canyon walls, unreachable, the chain of wooden ladders that once had led to them long since dust, like their inhabitants. How humans could have built such marvels in such a place and survived in them was something the imagination could not grasp, but Clyde Birdsong, the Ute, was proud of them. "My ancestors," he said, eyes glowing, "put those there. How's that for engineering, Captain Vane? And you call us savages . . ."

By now, each man knew the other and respected him. They were all fine white water men and outdoorsmen, tough, courageous, and reliable; but

Sara Raven was the real marvel. There was not a twist or turn of this river she did not know, not a channel nor a campsite. She was as much at home on the Colorado as a fish. But on occasions when she and Fargo found time to be alone, she was all woman, too.

And now they were sweeping down Glen Canyon, hemmed in by towering walls, some bearing ancient pictographs Birdsong's ancestors had climbed high up the walls to paint. In the immensity of this gorge, the faces of Vane and Michaelson lit up with the fervor of engineers. "What a place for a dam," Vane whispered. "Fargo, they'll put one here someday. They're bound to, if this region's ever to grow."

"The hell with you and your dams," Fargo growled, as they sat around the fire. "You want to settle up the whole country?"

"That's what the Corps of Engineers is for."

"Then the hell with the Corps of Engineers. Sometimes I can almost sympathize with Dogan. Leave something for us who like it wild."

"Don't worry. You'll be dead and gone before it's built."

"I hope so. I'm beginning to like this river. It's an outlaw river, and no wonder there's outlaws all along it. But at least they're men. What'll you bring in? Potbellied bankers, motor cars and ladies' sewing circles?"

"That's progress," said Vane.

Fargo answered him with an obscenity. Then he turned to Sara. "How many days to Cord's Park?"

Sara considered. In the firelight, she was, Fargo

thought, a beauty; somehow, at the end of every day's run, she found time to comb her hair until it glittered, and the damp clothing outlined every curve of her thoroughbred figure. "We can make the Crossing in three days."

"All right." He unfolded a map. "Then let's go over the layout again."

"It's just below where the San Juan River comes in, a few miles above the Arizona line. They used to call it the Crossing of the Fathers because, way I heard, the old Spanish missionaries used it. There's a side-canyon comes in from the west, and the Navajos used to cross the river there to raid the Mormons. So did the Utes, and they call it Ute Crossing sometimes. Anyhow, in the old days, the Mormons got tired of that, and they blasted the canyon closed so the Indians couldn't get down to the Colorado. It stayed closed until Dogan came along. He cleared a passage through it big enough for men on horseback. But it's still a rough trip through. Anyhow, the side canyon leads back up to Cord's Park. It's about a third the size of Brown's Hole, and there used to be some ranchers there. Dogan chased them out, he and Cord, and they named it after Cord, who came up with the idea in the first place. Dogan made it his headquarters, because there were warrants out for him in Wyoming, Utah, and Colorado, all three, but none in Arizona. In Cord's Park, he can dodge down to Arizona if the lawmen come and they can't touch him. So can most of the others with him who're in the same position."

"Go on," Fargo said.

"He gets in supplies through a front at Lee's

Crossing down in Arizona. The long riders on the southern Colorado buy from him at double price. He's gotten richer that way than he ever did robbing trains. He won't let anybody in there who's wanted in Arizona, so the authorities from there don't bother him. And . . . he's made a fort out of Cord's Park."

"I want your notebook and a pencil, Vane," Fargo said.

Vane passed them over. "Draw it," Fargo said, handing them to Sara and watched closely as she did.

"The only way in is up through the Crossing. Dogan has that guarded night and day, and he's planted dynamite there so he can blow it shut, if he has to. Otherwise, it's ringed in with cliffs, and there's only one back trail through, and that's guarded, too, and ready to be blown if necessary. He always keeps about three months supply of food there, and there's lots of water, so if anybody ever did move against him, it would take an army, like he says, and artillery, to blast him out, and there's no way anybody could bring artillery in."

"How many men there?"

"Anywhere from twenty to forty, depending who's come in for supplies. But the ones who live there are picked, Dogan's men, through and through. Twenty of those, anyhow, and all ready to fight and die if he says so."

"It's a fantastic operation," Michaelson said. "Who'd have thought that in these days, fifteen years in the Twentieth Century—"

"The Army has a saying," Fargo answered wryly.

"Old soldiers never die, they just fade away. That holds for outlaws, too, boy. You've made a living all your life with guns and a damned long lasso, you don't turn yourself in just because the country's settlin' up. You find some place you can keep on livin' and workin'. Dogan's smart. He saw the need, and he's provided that." His hands stroked the ever present Fox sawed-off on his lap, and he felt again that sick eagerness.

Sara's eyes caught the motion and perhaps the expression on his face. "Neal," she said quietly, "he couldn't have done it without that shotgun of his. He had a lot of rivals, but that shotgun took care of all of 'em. I . . . he's terribly dangerous with it."

"I know that," Fargo said. "Good."

"And I . . . thought I wanted him dead, wanted you to kill him. But . . . maybe that's not so important any more. Maybe there's some way to get Colonel Knight and his men out of there without you having to come up against Dogan and his shotgun."

"No," said Fargo. "There's no way."

"Neal."

"No way," he repeated. He took the sketch she had drawn, looked at it. It was all there: the cliff-rimmed bowl, two entrances, only one of which he was interested in. A scattering of cabins just inside the river entrance. "Where's Knight?"

"There." She pointed with the pencil. "He keeps Knight and the other four penned up in cabins, treats them like animals . . . makes sure they stay alive to bargain with, no more than that. I felt so sorry for them, the way he starved them . . ."

"But they can still move around."

"He gives them exercise every day, yes. Just enough to keep them going." She jabbed the pencil again. "His cabin's right there, the biggest one. He's got an Indian woman with him, a Ute. Just a girl; he found her and her family gathering food back in the hills and blasted her parents with his shotgun and took her the way he took my mother . . ."

Clyde Birdsong made a sound in his throat.

"Anyhow, at the river entrance, there are always four guards, day and night, two on either side of the canyon that leads up from the Colorado to the Park. And they can blow the entrance from each side."

"All right," Fargo said. "Well, we've lost three rifles in the rapids. We can replace those and one to spare."

Vane said, "Fargo. What have you got in mind?"

"We make two more runs in daylight. The last we make at night."

"Impossible!" Vane exploded. "You can't run this kind of water at night!"

Fargo looked at Sara. Comprehending, she smiled faintly. "I can. I've traveled this part so many times I could do it with my eyes closed."

"We run at night," Fargo repeated. "Then it's up to me and Birdsong to get the rifles. After that, it's up to you and the rest to cover us, and—here's what I've got in mind." He spread the sketch Sara had drawn before them and began to talk.

Two more days, running down Glen Canyon.

132

There were rapids, but none so fierce as those they had already navigated. It would almost have been a pleasure cruise, thought Fargo, if—he watched the canyon rims—if they were lucky, and there were no guards there. Undoubtedly, through Cord, Dogan knew there was another expedition on the river. Likely he and Cord had set an approximate date for its arrival at the Crossing—and its destruction. What he could not know, unless somebody had ridden a horse with wings, was that Cord was dead, Garfield dead, Sara freed, and that the expedition had hurtled downstream faster than any other in the Colorado's history. He was expecting Cord to deliver it to him in a package on a certain date; they were far ahead of time, and the package, thought Fargo wryly, was a ticking time bomb. Still, he was always watchful.

But it was all right. They found a campsite in some willows on a sandbar, hid the boats. Sara said, "The last run's easy. Only a few hours. I could have you at the Crossing by midnight."

"That's good," Fargo said. "Absolutely the right time. Now. Tell us about the cliffs again." He and Birdsong listened carefully as she did, and Fargo felt his palms begin to sweat. There was very little he had faced in his life that truly frightened him, but he had one in-built fear that he had never completely overcome: a fear of heights. He could face shotguns, Colts, knives; but high places strained his nerves. Still, there was no help for it; the fear would be there, but he would have to ignore it to do what he must do.

When she had finished, he wiped his hands on his

pants. "That's all right," he said. "That's good. Birdsong—?"

The Ute smiled, teeth gleaming in the fireshine. "I've got it, Fargo. Nothing to it."

John Michaelson stood up. "Fargo, I don't understand. I'm an experienced mountain climber. Why Birdsong? Why not me?"

Before Fargo could answer, the Ute bounced to his feet. "John, I'll tell you why. I'm an Indian, you're a white man. This is my country, it isn't yours."

"I don't see—"

"I grew up in this country," Birdsong went on softly. "Climbing cliffs like those. Stalking animals. I've seen the time when whether we ate or starved depended on whether we could get close enough to a lousy jack rabbit to kill it with a stick or the only bullet we owned among us. Myself, when I was fourteen, I stalked a deer and jumped on its back and cut its throat, and it never knew I was there until my knife dug in. I know what Fargo wants and I can do it. Four years at Carlisle didn't take the Injun out of me. Fargo and I are going hunting —in the canyon country. This time it's men. That makes no difference. A man is like a deer, only duller, sleepier. And besides—didn't you hear Miss Raven the other night? Dogan has taken a Ute girl. No, John. I go with Fargo." Suddenly, as if embarrassed at talking too much, he turned, strode into the willows.

Fargo said quietly: "Birdsong's the man I want. But you'll all get your chances. Now, see to your weapons. Tomorrow night, we make the run."

And then he broke the shotgun and meticulously cleaned and oiled it.

Like shadows, the boats glided through the moonless dark in the bottom of the great canyon. In the stern of each, a downpointed flashlight guided those behind. Sara, in the bow of the lead boat, navigated expertly through water slack by comparison with that which they had run already. Behind her, shotgun slung, rifle across his lap, Fargo used the oars to brake and guide as necessary.

They kept in close to canyon walls. Once a huge rock hurtled down, but it landed in midstream with a mighty splash. Fargo ignored it; if there were another one, it might mean they were spotted and under attack; but none came.

Normally, just before going into combat, he was cool, almost icy. Tonight, though, his hands sweated on the oars. He kept thinking about the cliffs. Well, he told himself, this was when he would really earn his pay. Anybody could take ordinary risks; you were a man when you overcame the kind of fear that shrank your belly and wet your hands and went on to do what had to be done regardless.

Then he was aware of the boat changing direction. Sara's whisper came through the darkness. "Neal, we're almost there."

"You're putting in?"

"Long enough to let you out. The path is right there—" she pointed. "Where that big willow grows."

"All right," Fargo said. The boat grated on sand;

135

he stepped out, shrugged off the bandolier of Winchester cartridges, passed Sara the rifle.

"I'll run past the crossing," she whispered, "let Birdsong out on the other side. Then wait 'til you come back."

"Unless you hear gunfire," Fargo said. "If you do, run on downriver and hole up. Birdsong—"

The Ute put out a small, strong, hard hand. "Good luck, Fargo."

"Same to you. Don't forget the signal."

"Right. Two coyote barks, then a third."

"That's it," Fargo said, and he faded into the willows at the foot of the sheer cliff, hundreds of feet high, that towered over him. Not far from where he hid, the side canyon made a gap of greater darkness, a slot spilling down from the highlands above. He watched the boats glide past, then they were lost in darkness. He squatted in the willows, shielded the final cigar he lit with his hand, smoked patiently until enough time had elapsed for Birdsong to be in place. Then, somewhat reluctantly, he ground out his cigar.

The side canyon was not the only way into Cord's Park. After the Mormons had blasted it shut, Indians had still come down to the river and crossed here, but on foot, not on horseback. On either side of the smaller canyon, they had worked trails down the cliff faces. Not trails, really, so much as a tenuous series of hand and footholds; but they could be climbed: Sara had seen men do it. Now it was up to Fargo to mount one and to Birdsong to climb the other, and when they reached the rims above, where the guards were, waiting to blow the dynamite in case of attack ... Fargo adjusted his shotgun sling, the bandolier of shells, checked the Batangas knife in its sheath. Well, it was time to go. Five hundred feet, maybe more, he judged. And no way out of it. He moved behind the big willow, surveyed the rock with his hand, and then he found the trail. His gut knotted and his heart sank, as he groped up the wall. A few inches here, a few there, a place to dig in a hand or toes, and all of it weathered over decades, smoothed and slippery. He spat dryly, hooked a booted toe in the first niche, hoisted himself.

At first, it was not so bad. Somehow it all went together. When you had one foothold, you reached for another and it was, miraculously, there, and a place for hands to grab as well. Ten or twenty feet above the ground, there was nothing to it. But ... forty, fifty. He inched higher. And slowly but surely the old fear pierced him.

It was like pain. People died from pain because they let it worry them. The thing to do with pain was bear it. If your wound was fatal, pain made no difference; that was true, too, if it was not. Handle fear the same way, ignore it ... don't let it kill you uselessly.

He bit his lip. He was sixty feet up the cliff, now, with seven times that height to climb. Those damned foot and handholes were almost, but not quite, big enough. He paused, felt for next grasp, found it, hoisted himself another yard. It took an effort of will, but he made it. Then he was a hundred feet above the ground, and that seemed forever: the sandbar a tiny lozenge, the river a rushing fury, its rocks waiting to catch him. His head swam, his mouth was dry and panic hit him. His mouth was dry, his knees trembling, and his nails broke on the rock as his fingers dug into the scanty handhold. For that interval, he was capable of going neither up nor down. He only clung there, heart pounding, gut full of sickness.

Then he sucked in a long breath. Fury rose in him at his own cowardice. He thought of his contempt for people who wanted to live forever, people who feared cold steel or lead or bad horses or wild cattle or all the other ways you could get killed. He would not be ranked with them. His pride took over, cold and fierce, and he scrabbled for another handhold, and another. He had mastered the fear now and the sickness. He still hated what he had to do, but it no longer touched him. Mechanically, he went on climbing, not a person, only a machine.

Two hundred feet, three. Then, terrifyingly, a gap. He searched in all directions, pinned there like a spider on a wall, and could find no place to get a foot or handhold. He dared not look down into the sickening depths beneath. *There has to be one!* he thought—*somewhere*. Balancing on his toes, swinging partly into space, he reached higher. Then he found it, a crevice into which he could get his fingers. He explored, found another near it. He would have to hoist himself up one-handed, then reach for the other. With his fingers there, find another hold above and then dig in his feet. He swallowed hard, reached up, sank fingers into the niche, let go, and then he was dangling by one hand high above the Colorado. Frantically he scrabbled with the other.

After endless seconds, it found a grip. Fargo closed his eyes, hung there by both hands for a minute, not daring to brace his feet too hard against the canyon wall. His arm muscles shrieked with strain.

"Shit," he said aloud, bitterly, let go with his lower hand, swung by one and reached up again. He found another hold, pulled with all his strength. This time his left foot found purchase, and now he had two hands and a foothold.

Once more straining upward, he found another handhold, and he relaxed. That had been a gap, but now maybe it would be all right. He hoisted, sought again for purchase—and it *was* all right. The foot and handholds were where they should be now, and he went up with comparative speed. Above him, he could see the canyon rim, a streak against the sky. Below, the river raced and rumbled, and the boulders waited. If a man fell now, he thought, he'd have a long time to anticipate what it would be like when he hit—.

But only another hundred feet . . . surely he could make that, despite quivering arms and legs. Climbing on he gained another thirty, forty . . . the rim was tantalizingly close. Only fifty feet now, and . . . he closed the space to thirty, twenty; then, four hundred feet and more above the river, he froze and pressed himself against the hard, cold stone of the canyon wall.

The silhouetted figure of a man stalked along the

rim. Paused, came back. Fargo could see it in weird perspective, enormous boots and legs, diminishing waist, torso and head. Saw the glint of fleeting moonlight on the metal of a rifle barrel. Dogan took no chances! His men watched these trails!

Eyes closed, Fargo hung there for endless seconds. Then he knew what he had to do and went on up. Another ten feet, twenty, soundless as a cat, taking his time. Now the edge of the rimrock was only ten feet overhead. He heard the footsteps of the man pacing past. The guard moved twenty, thirty yards along the rim, halted, lit a cigarette. Fargo found his grips and squirreled up the last few yards. Then, clinging by both hands and one foot, he was just below the edge. He waited there. The man paced by again. Two feet, Fargo judged, from the rim of the sheer drop to the rocks below.

Fargo freed a hand, dangled, unslung his shotgun. Hanging precariously, head just below the rim, he waited. The man came back again with bored, careless paces. As he went by, Fargo surged up, rammed the shotgun between his legs, twisted. The man grunted, thrown off balance. Then he fell outwards into space, just missing Fargo. He was so surprised he didn't even scream until he was halfway down, and the river almost swallowed that sound. Fargo, expecting it, caught the splash he made, then he seized the edge of rimrock and was scrambling over. On solid ground, he fought back the impulse to vomit. Instead, he slung the shotgun, drew the Batangas knife, flicked back the handles, exposed the blade, and lay flat, waiting.

Footsteps, and he had expected them. "Hey,

Kelly—" Another shadowy figure, rifle up. It walked right by Fargo. "Kelly—?"

From behind the cover of a pile of rocks, Fargo came erect. He moved soundlessly across three yards, knife blade glinting in the moonlight. His left arm clamped hard around the guard's neck; his right hand thrust and thrust again. Teeth bit down on the hand clamping off a scream. Fargo ignored them and killed the man with a final stroke. When the body was limp, he let it drop, then took from the corpse a pistol and a Winchester. He sheathed the Batangas knife, ran low across some open ground, threw himself flat on the rim of the side canyon.

He waited there for what seemed endless seconds. He had climbed a half thousand foot cliff and killed two men, and he had never wanted a drink more in his life. He let the reaction pass away, and then it came, from across the side canyon: the barking of a coyote.

Fargo's lips peeled back from his teeth in a wolfish snarl. He answered with a coyote's bark, perfectly rendered. Then, keeping low in the moonlight flooding the rim, he searched for the detonator.

He found it, a push-type box, designed to send a spark along wires to the capped dynamite below. He ripped loose the wires, threw the detonator into darkness. Then, in the shelter of a boulder, he waited for a long time, until the coyote call came again. He answered that one, too. Then he ran along the side-canyon's rim.

A well-worn path carried him down to the bowl below: Cord's Park. Where the side-canyon debouched into it, he paused in the shelter of a boulder, and then, presently, saw movement in the darkness opposite. He hissed: "Birdsong."

"Fargo? I'm here." The Ute came to join him behind the house-sized rock. He was breathing hard, but there was excitement, a wild kind of joy, in his words. "No trouble, none at all. The Old Ones cut a fine path—and those guards were easier than deer! I've got two rifles and three pistols. Now what?"

"I lost a rifle. Now we wait," Fargo said, and they hunkered down in the shadows behind the boulder.

A long time passed, during which neither moved nor spoke. Then, well after midnight, there was sound: a rock rolled in the side-canyon below. Fargo and Birdsong tensed as shadowy figures appeared, Vane's blocky form in the forefront. Fargo hissed Vane's name.

They came together behind the boulder. "Sara's waiting with the boats," Vane whispered. "Did it go all right?"

"Right on schedule. Now, get your men up on the rim to cover us, while Birdsong and I go in and find Knight and his bunch, let 'em out and arm 'em. We'll try to sneak back out without shooting, but if there's gunfire, pick your targets and open up."

"All right," Vane began. "I—" His voice chopped off as from the river far below there came a high, shrill, thready sound—unmistakably a woman's scream.

Fargo whirled. "Sara!" he rasped. And all at once he knew it had gone wrong, bad wrong. He raised the shotgun, but even as he did so, a voice boomed out through the night from the rim not far above their heads. It echoed and re-echoed in the stillness, gaining volume, so that finally it seemed to come through a megaphone. "All right!" it roared, and echoes repeated. "Lay down those guns, you men, you hear? You're covered by twenty rifles and a sawed-off! Lay down those guns!"

And then, still with that hollow, echoing boom, it added: "This is Dogan speaking. Double-Barrel Dogan!" And, mockingly, it added: "Welcome, Fargo, to Cord's Park! It's your last stop on the way to Hell!"

There was a moment, then, where every man of Fargo's party froze. Michaelson made a sound in his throat, raised his gun. "God damn—."

Fargo said, bitterly, "Ease off, John. They've got us cold." Because he had seen them, now. They were on both rims of the side-canyon, aimed rifles catching moonlight gleams. And there were more of them coming up the canyon trail, plugging the narrow passage that led into Dogan's stronghold, and others appearing now from boulders ahead, where they'd been hidden. They were boxed in on all flanks, and there was no escape, no fighting back. Somehow he had led the entire party into a trap.

"Lay down your guns or you'll be dead in thirty seconds!" the voice boomed. "Do what I say and some of you can live! You hear me?"

"We hear you," Fargo yelled. And then, because they were outnumbered and caught cold and there was nothing else to do, he unslung his Fox and then fished out his Colt and put them both aside and raised his hands. Staring at him, the others fol-

143

lowed suit, as armed men closed in on them and more menaced them from the walls above. From down the canyon, Sara screamed again, but the sound pinched off quickly.

"We surrender," Fargo called bitterly.

"You'd damned well better," the voice boomed. Then rock slid, as a man descended the trail from the rim into the canyon. He landed lightly, after sliding a few yards, regained his balance, turned, and as he strode forward, entered a shaft of moonlight. Fargo stared at the leveled sawed-off Greener, which, if both triggers were pulled, would kill every man in the party.

"Dogan," he said.

"Me, in the flesh," Dogan answered. He was a tall, narrow-waisted silhouette against the darkness. "Pick up their hardware, men, and bring them in. We've got a lot of business to transact 'tween now and daylight."

Chapter VIII

"You bitch!" Dogan snarled, and, backhanded, hit Sara again with all his strength. Her head snapped around and she staggered back to collapse in a corner of the room. Dogan grinned and whirled, shotgun leveled. "Goes against the grain? Too damn bad, gentlemen. Just don't move."

His headquarters were a barroom and store not much different from the one in Brown's Hole. He moved the Greener back and forth, and when, under its muzzles, no one stirred, his grin widened. Still keeping the shotgun aimed, he went to a table, sat down behind it, like a judge facing a mass of accused men—or condemned ones.

"Well," Dogan said. He drank from a bottle on the table, and as he did so, Fargo had time, in the flickering light of the kerosene lamps spotted around the room, to size him up.

His face was almost the one Fargo had seen in pictures supposed to be of his corpse—like a hatchet blade, narrow, big-nosed, thin-mouthed and with a pointed chin. His eyes were blue, beneath dark brows, and they were like twin gas flames. His hair, beneath the tipped back sombrero, was longer than Fargo's and just as white, but with age; Dogan, now, would be just past fifty. But years had not sapped the vigor of his frame, tall as Fargo's own, more slender, yet still with the quickness and power of a panther. He wore a flannel shirt, Levis, boots, and no side-arms at all. He did not need them, for Fargo knew he would never be without the Greener, whose ten-gauge bores menaced all of them.

Dogan's flame-jet eyes roamed over the captives, every man of the expedition, and came to rest on Fargo. Dogan's lips peeled back from bad teeth in a grin. "And you're still wondering how," he said. "The great Neal Fargo, and he's wondering how Double-Barrel Dogan caught him like a sucker in a fish-net."

Fargo didn't answer. He was looking at Sara, battered, limp in the corner. She had been almost dragged up the canyon-gate to Cord's Park by two more armed men, and although they had already roughed her up, Dogan had worked her over savagely. And there was nothing anyone could do to stop him, menaced by his shotgun and the revolvers and pistols of a dozen other men.

"So I'll tell you," Dogan said. "Heliograph."

Fargo snapped around, suddenly alert.

"Gets you, huh? Never counted on that? The

river, yes, or horseback, but not on mirrors." Dogan leaned back in his chair, but he kept his hand on the riot gun. "The sunshine telegraph, just like the Army used chasing Apaches. I'm organized, Fargo. It's part of the service people pay me for. I've got heliograph stations set up every ten miles back in the badlands. We use Morse Code and the sun and mirrors do the rest. Fast as telegraph. And you didn't think of that."

"No, I didn't." Fargo looked at Sara.

"And she didn't tell you. Well, she didn't know. It was something I figured she was better off not knowing. But it's there. Ten hours after you killed Garfield and went off with her in Brown's Hole, we knew it here. We've watched you all the way downriver. Knew when you were coming in here, let you come. Cost me four men, but they were way behind on the books anyhow, and I had to get rid of 'em. Worth it to let you deliver yourself and all your crew."

His hand stroked the shotgun. "But it was worth it, even if they hadn't of been. Had men staked out all up and down the approaches; you walked in slick as a whistle. And now . . . now I got more bargaining power. You and the Injun don't count, Fargo, but that still leaves six soldiers and sailors and bigwigs of one kind or another. Add those to Knight and his people, it gives me eleven valuable bargainin' counters if it ever comes to that. Plus, I got Sara back, three good river boats and—I appreciate it, Fargo. You not thinkin' of those mirrors."

"I should have," Fargo said bitterly.

"No reason for you to. Nobody uses heliograph any more, now that the telegraph runs everywhere. Only us owlhooters." He shoved back his chair, stood up, and raised the Greener. "Injun," he said to Birdsong. "Move over there against the wall."

Birdsong faced him defiantly. "Go to hell, white man."

Dogan came out from behind the table. He walked up to within two feet of Birdsong. "You dirty Ute," he said. "I just rubbed out a woman of your tribe because she was so troublesome. Killed her, you understand? Good thing Sara came back; I need another woman. Now—over there against the wall."

"Go to hell," Birdsong rasped again.

Like a drum-major's baton, the shotgun whirled in Dogan's hands. The stock struck Birdsong, and he staggered back, brought up against the big room's log wall. Dogan pivoted, and now the gun was reversed again, stock by his hip, barrels pointed. "Bang," he said. "You're dead." And he pulled one trigger.

The shotgun's roar was deafening in the little room. From the corner, Sara made a thin sound. Birdsong made none at all. Caught at close range by nine buckshot, he was nearly cut in two. His mutilated body simply collapsed silently, dead before it struck the floor.

Dogan whirled, and now the gun was lined on Fargo. Fargo tensed, but Dogan only grinned. "Neat, eh?" he said. "You'd appreciate it, being a shotgun man."

148

He waited for some reaction, and when none was forthcoming, he said, "Jonas. Bring me that Fox."

A squat man came forward with Fargo's shotgun and bandolier. Dogan dropped into his chair again, laid the Greener aside. He examined Fargo's shotgun, and his eyes glowed, his face lit. "Judas, what a fine weapon. The Greener's good, but this engravin'—it must have cost a fortune." He broke the gun, saw that it was fully loaded, closed it once more, and now it was the Fox he leveled at Fargo. "Jonas. Take the rest of 'em away. Shut 'em up with Knight and the others and mount a guard. Leave me alone. All of you leave me alone with Fargo."

"Yes, sir," Jonas said. "Move out, you men."

Vane protested, but all those guns pointed at him stifled it. Hands raised, the men filed out, covered by more than two guns each. "Ross!" Dogan barked.

A trailing man turned. Dogan jerked his thumb. "Her. Sara. Take her in the bedroom and lock her in and stand guard outside the window."

Sara was past fighting as the man jerked her to her feet. He shoved her behind the bar, through a door. He emerged, slid a bar, then went out. Now the barroom was empty, save for Dogan and Neal Fargo.

Dogan fished a cigar from his pocket, clamped it in his mouth. "You want a drink," he said pleasantly, "there's a bottle on the bar."

Fargo looked: there was. "Obliged," he said, went to it drank, Dogan covering him with the Fox.

He smacked his lips and drank again and set down the bottle and leaned against the bar.

"Neal Fargo," Dogan said. "That's one thing I've hated about pretending to be dead." He lit the cigar. "You know, there was a time when I was top man with a sawed-off and everybody knew it. But now I'm dead, you see? Officially. Actually, it was that stupid brother of mine. But . . . I got no rep left. There ain't what you would call a shotgun man no more, except maybe you."

Not speaking, Fargo helped himself to another drink. He was very tired, and he would need all the lift he could get.

"It's a goddam shame," Dogan went on. "People don't seem to know it, but it was the shotgun did the business. They gave shotguns to Texas Rangers before they had repeating pistols. No lawman ever kept a town tamed without shotguns. Wyatt Earp used 'em in Wichita and Dodge and Ellsworth and Tombstone. No stage line would ever have made a bullion run without a shotgun guard, and they were standard weapons for express messengers on trains. To hell with your *pistoleros!* You give me six slugs to throw or eighteen buckshot and I'll take the buckshot every time." He looked down at the Fox. "*To Fargo from Roosevelt.* No wonder this is such a purty gun. You've used it on a lot of people, huh?"

"I have," said Fargo.

"How long, originally, the barrels."

"Thirty-two inches."

"Goose gun," Dogan said. "Special made. And you cut all that off?"

"I don't hunt geese," Fargo said.

Dogan laughed throatily. Then he sobered. "No. You were hunting me. Too bad, Fargo. But I'll enjoy the gun. You know, I don't allow anybody in my territory to tote a sawed-off except me." He drank again from the bottle on the table, and his eyes shadowed. "It's funny. How my whole life has been built around this Greener, here. I was a damned good stagecoach guard once. I risked my life for Wells-Fargo and other lines a lot more'n once, and this company-issue Greener took its toll of bandits. But were they grateful? No, sir! I got sixty a month for ridin' shotgun! And one day it hit me! I was on the wrong end ..."

He rubbed his face. "Funny thing was, I'd just asked for a ten-dollar raise. If they'd given it to me, I'da been happy, but they turned me down. And it riled me, you know? And that was when I decided which way my stick would float." He laughed. "And since then, this Wells-Fargo Greener has taken back that raise from Wells-Fargo many times over. I've tried to explain all that to a lot of people, but none of 'em could understand. But you do, don't you? You know that when you use a sawed-off, you do it close up, and it's them or you, no other way."

"That's how it is," Fargo said.

Dogan rolled the cigar across his mouth. "And Garfield's dead," he said. "And I need a man up in Brown's Hole to run things. A man that won't get blubber-fat and careless like Garfield. And a man that takes to Sara and that she takes to—I saw the way you looked at her when I laid one on her. Fargo, you work for hire. What kind of hire?"

"Fifteen, twenty thousand a job," Fargo said, catching the drift.

"How many jobs a year?"

"Two, anyhow."

"Good pay. But I could guarantee you fifty a year, not near as much risk, and Sara—after I've found me another woman for my own use. How does that sound to you?"

Fargo fished in his shirt pocket, brought out a tin waterproof box that held his last cigar. He put the cigar between his teeth and lit it. "Do I get my Fox back?"

"No. I told you, nobody totes a sawed-off but me. You don't need it anyhow; you're good enough with that Colt or a knife." He leaned forward, still keeping the shotgun leveled, thoroughly the professional. "You and me can get along, Fargo. There ain't that much difference between us. I know your rep; I know everything goes on from Wyoming to Sonora. I know you're wild, like me, like these men along the river. But you're getting old, you can't go on straining forever to earn the hard dollar. And when you get too old, where you gonna go? These Army bastards, scientists, whatever, they're tryin' to take it all away from us, men like you and me. They open up the back country, what becomes of us?"

"I don't know," Fargo said.

"Well, you got until the sun comes up to think about it. Then somebody dies. You or that man called Vane."

Fargo stiffened. "What?"

"You're either with me or against me. If you're

152

with me, you run Brown's Hole, make a big stake, have Sara, and if the heat goes on, we'll head out for Argentina. If you're against me, you die; it's that simple. And the only way I can be sure you're with me is to make your stakes the same as mine. I kill you . . . or you kill Captain Vane."

Fargo said, "I don't—"

"I thought you were smart. I'd put no man in a place of trust until he'd proved himself. You kill Vane, in cold blood, before Knight and all the rest, and then we're playing the same game. You can't afford to be caught either. So you've got to be on my side. It's a simple test, Fargo. Simpler than assaying gold. You kill Vane, you're on the hook. You refuse, I kill you. Nothing simpler than that. When you get my age, you simplify everything."

With a certain admiration, Fargo stared at the man behind the shotguns. Dogan overlooked no bet. But, after all, this was the cold intelligence that had sacrificed his own brother to clear himself. And what he said was true: if Fargo were forced to kill Vane before witnesses, he was bound to Dogan forever. For then it became a matter of his own survival to make sure that neither Knight nor any of the others would ever testify against him. Now he understood how Dogan had established his rule over the Colorado; and once more that sick lust to challenge such a shotgun man stirred in him.

But there was no challenging Dogan's dead drop with the Fox.

"I got to think about it," he said.

"Sure. Naturally you got to think about it. But

153

there ain't but one answer. Either you are alive come dinner time, or you are dead. Me, what I've heard about you, I figure you'd rather be alive. After all, you use a shotgun, and a man that does that is smart, smarter than the regular. He's already thought about the odds."

He twitched Fargo's Fox, just enough to be emphatic. "Now, sit down at yonder table, not too close. Until Vane's dead, you're my enemy. After that, you got to be my friend. But I'm shut off here and you've been around outside, and there's a lot I want to know . . ."

* * *

For Neal Fargo, the next three hours were a nightmare, and yet they had a fascination. Menaced by the bores of his own weapon, he sat across the room from Dogan and heard reminiscences of days long turned to legend; in return, Dogan picked his brains, demanding information on new weapons and law enforcement procedures on the outside. Every question had its point, and Fargo knew he was in the presence of a towering, ruthless intelligence. Not since the Colonel had he met so forceful, brilliant, and dangerous a man.

And that, he thought, was what the choice was boiling down to. Serve one master or the other. And the Fox twelve-gauge was somehow the symbol of that choice. Yield it up, kill Vane, and live. Or stay loyal to the man who'd given it to him—and die. No third way.

"This execution," he asked finally, as dawn shafted light through dirty windows. "Vane's. How would it work?"

"Nothing to it. We march 'em out, all of 'em, so they can see it. Knight and his men, that crew you brought in. And . . ." His mouth curled. "Sara. She's got to see it, too, so she knows where everybody stands. Then, in full view of all, you shoot Vane."

Fargo rubbed his eyes with weariness. At last, slowly, he said, "All right. Looks like there's no way around it. I've had worse deals offered. I'll do it. Give me back my shotgun and one round."

"No," said Dogan. "You think I'm a fool? Let you turn nine buckshot on me and my men? Uh-uh. You get your Colt and one round. You can put it spang against Vane's head. That hollow-point ought to blow it plumb apart."

"And then do I get my shotgun back?"

"You get all your weapons back except the Fox. My rule holds. Nobody has a shotgun in this outfit but me. It's my edge, Fargo—and you're the man to know about that."

Fargo looked at him wryly, almost with contempt. "So you're that scared of me."

"I ain't scared of any man ever drew on a boot." He took a drink from the bottle near him. "Oh, don't think I ain't thought about it. From the days when I first started to hear the stories about Neal Fargo and his sawed-off, I had an itch—you know what I mean?" Before Fargo could answer, he grinned. "You damned well know; I can see it in your eyes. I . . . wanted a chance to come up against you. But it can't be that way. No. I keep your shot-gun."

Fargo was silent for a moment. Then he had a drink from his own bottle. "Dogan, it wouldn't work."

"What?" Dogan's gas-jet eyes seemed to intensify their blueness.

"It don't matter what kind of deal we make— I'd have to have my shotgun before we could work together."

"Looks to me like you ought to be satisfied with your life." But Fargo saw at once that the quick intelligence followed his drift immediately.

He stood up, began to pace. He'd been sitting too long, needed to be limber, tuned. He had one last card to play; its only chance of taking the pot hinged on Dogan's mind, the way it worked, the slant of it. They were weapons men, both of them: a breed, for better or worse, to whom guns, fine guns, were more important than women or money. A cheap gun, like a sluttish woman or a counterfeit dollar, was an abomination, to be despised. But a fine one was worth killing for, or even dying for. It was a kind of madness, Fargo knew: the madness of the gunman. But he and Dogan were both caught up in it.

"It wouldn't work," he said, "because you know that I'd never rest or settle into harness without my shotgun. I've carried it too long, it's pulled me out of too many spots, I've killed too many men with it before they could kill me. It's part of me, Dogan, and I'll have to have it back."

156

"You won't get it," Dogan said. "I'll just kill you and be done with it."

"Do that," Fargo said. "And that shotgun will cost you more than you ever paid for any weapon in your life."

Dogan sat up straight. "You lost me there."

Fargo halted, leaned against the bar, toyed with half a dozen bottle corks left over from the opening of whiskey. He picked up several, tossed them idly in his hands. Then he turned, biting his lower lip thoughtfully, releasing it. "All right," he said. "I'll put it this way. You need me. You need me bad enough to give me back my Fox." His voice roughened. "You been shut up here for a long time, Dogan. You got no idea what's going on outside, how it's changed. Why do you think they sent two expeditions down the Colorado? They're moving in on you, harder and faster than you ever dreamed. And when both expeditions disappear, they'll really be riled up and come in even harder. You can't last here. The time will come, a year, two or four from now when you'll have to fight a rearguard action and move out below the border. Without me, you'll never make it."

"I've made it this far."

"You've been lucky. But when they come the next time, they'll come in force. It'll be the Army or the State Militias. And you won't stand them off with rifles and shotguns. Because they'll have machine guns and pack howitzers, and they'll move in and blast you out of these breaks from miles away, and you'll never get a chance to use that Greener of yours—"

He strode toward Dogan. Dogan tilted up the Fox. "Hold it, Fargo."

"That famous Greener," Fargo said. "I want to see it."

Dogan said, "You keep your hands off of it."

"All I want's a look. But let that ride. My point is this. Dogan, you're obsolete. Except for close-in fighting, so are our shotguns. This is the machine gun and cannon age, and you don't know a damned thing about either one."

"And you do . . ."

"All there is to know. I know where to get machine guns and pack howitzers and Hotchkiss repeating two-pounders and how to set 'em up and operate 'em. I know how to fortify this place you got so nobody can ever come past Brown's Hole with a full-scale Army. And I know how to fight the rear-guard action that'll have to be fought and where we go when we pull out."

"And where's that?" Dogan's eyes were keen.

"Mexico. I've been running guns to Villa, I know all those people down there. I can get guns for us, and I can set up a hideout when we need it. Garfield was a slob, a nothing. Whatever I am, I ain't that. Anyhow, write it on your slate: without me, your days are numbered. You can't stand off an army with a Greener and a Fox. If I throw in with you, I'll show you the new way of fighting. But I won't do it unless I get my shotgun."

"Then, like I said, I guess I got to kill you."

"You do that, you shorten your own life. I'll take your proposition just like you laid it down. My only term is that I get my shotgun back."

Dogan frowned. "I don't know. I—" He broke off. Suddenly Sara's screams rose from inside the room; she began to hammer at the door. "Dogan! Fargo! Take this swine out of here!"

Dogan jumped up, face contorting, raised Fargo's Fox. He cast a quick glance at Fargo, grinned. "Sounds like Jonas has got carried away. Musta crawled in through the window. He oughta know better than that. I'm gonna see to him. All right—" Sara was still screaming. Fargo heard her snarl, "turn loose of me, you bastard!"

"All right," Dogan said. "Look at the Greener. It's empty and you got no ten-gauge shells. And try no tricks, because there's guards front and back." He strode around the bar, Fox tilted up, found a key, unlocked the door, went in.

Fargo moved swiftly, smoothly to the table where the Greener lay, the use-slickened old hammer gun that had taken so many lives. His eyes ranged over its barrels as his hands moved deftly, and his mouth twisted. Damascus Twist. Of course. All the real old guns were. There were two ways of making a shotgun barrel. The modern way was to ream one out of a solid piece of steel. Years before, though, they had laminated curling pieces of hot iron around a core and forged those pieces together so smoothly that they appeared to be a single piece of metal. But, fine as the workmanship in any gun made of Damascus Twist was, there was a weakness—a good eye could always see the laminations.

Then he heard Dogan snarl something, Sara

scream, and man and woman alike were back in the bar room, Dogan holding Sara by a hand knotted in her hair, his shotgun poked into her ribs. "You slut! I oughta kill you!"

He threw her across the room, and she landed in a corner not far from Birdsong's body. Fargo laid down the Greener, and it was broken open, still empty, and Dogan's eyes took that in quickly, then went back to Sara. "You know what she did?" he rasped. "Kicked up all that fuss to give you some kind of chance. Thought maybe it would distract me and let you jump me. And Jonas was still outside!" He whirled toward Sara. "Girl!" he rasped, "you been nothing but a problem to me ever since I come here. Well, you ain't my flesh and blood. No reason why I can't tame you like I tamed your mama and all the rest. You'll stay with me a while, and then if you behave, Fargo can have you. But if you ever try another trick like that, I'll cut you up so you won't recognize yourself!" He turned to Fargo, still caught up in rage.

"All right," he snapped. "My mind's made up. You get your shotgun back. One round in it, to kill Vane with. And don't try to trick me, because—" He broke Fargo's shotgun, drew out the left shell. Laid it on the table, picked up his own Greener, dug in his pockets, rammed in two fat rounds, snapped it shut. "Once Vane is dead, I'll give you the rest of your ammunition. I'll know you're bound to me then."

"Fair enough," Fargo said. "I never asked no more. I'll kill Vane for you. And let's get it over with. I want my shotgun back."

160

"We'll get it over with!" Dogan snapped. "Jonas!"

Almost immediately, the squat man appeared.

Dogan gestured toward Sara. "Pick this slut up and watch her. She tried to make your name mud, so don't let her get away. And tell Forester to have the men bring out Knight and all the rest. Line 'em up alongside the store."

"Sure, Mr. Dogan," Jonas said. He went to Sara, seized her hand, jerked her up and hammerlocked her again. "You come with me."

She screamed curses at him, but he forced her out the door. Dogan went to the table, picked up the Greener, leveled it on Fargo. Then tossed him the Fox. "There it is," he rasped. "One round, nine buckshot. Use it on Vane. If you try to use it on me, you'll never leave this park, because twenty men will blow you down, if I don't do it first with the Greener."

"You think I'm a complete idiot?" Fargo asked.

"We'll see," Dogan said. "I almost wish you were. Then I'd have an excuse . . . No. No, I need you, I got to use you. But move out. I want to see you kill Vane."

They went outside, into the green, sunlit bowl hemmed in by mountains. Dogan kept the Greener trained on Fargo, who carried very delicately the Fox with its one round in the chamber. He sucked in clean draughts of morning air, cleared his lungs and head. In that moment, looking around, he felt kinship with Dogan. This was a clean, wild place; it could stay like this, or people like Vane could bring in their dams and bankers and sewing circles . . .

"Just rest easy," Dogan said, keeping the Greener trained, Fargo's Colt and knife in his waistband. "They'll be along directly. Minute you raise that shotgun off the ground, where you got it pointed, I'll be tempted to shoot."

"We wouldn't be dealing if I was fool enough to do that." Fargo's voice was almost angry. "One more man, what do you think that means to me? What counts for me is staying alive." Then he heard the shuffling of many feet. Careful to keep the Fox downpointed, he turned.

They came, sixteen of them, armed, Dogan's men. And between their twin ranks marched another eleven. Six of those were the crew Fargo had run the Colorado with, Vane in the lead, shoulders squared, eyes forward. Behind him shambled five human wrecks, clad in rags, covered with sores. Fargo had to look a long time before he recognized the gangling skeleton leading that last contingent as the brawny Lieutenant Knight of the old Rough Riders.

But Knight recognized him at once. "Sergeant Fargo!"

"Shut up!" Jonas said and slapped Knight across the face. Knight slumped, subsided.

"Put that Vane fella up against the wall," Dogan ordered.

"Right." Two men hustled Captain Vane against the side of the saloon. Vane pressed his back against the logs with ramrod straightness and stared at Fargo. "What's happening? What's this all about?"

"I got to kill you," Fargo said. "It's the only way I can stay alive. I'm throwing in with Dogan."

"I see." Vane's voice was contemptuous. "Well, my first appraisal was correct, eh? Water seeks its own level, and so do gunmen . . ."

"Knock it off," Fargo said and hit him. Sara screamed.

"Fargo, you can't—!"

"Somebody shut her up," Fargo rasped. He backed a pace. Everything was very still as he raised the Fox. Pressed it against Vane's chest.

"All right," Vane said harshly. "I've never been under fire, but I suppose this is the ultimate test. You might get word to my family somehow that I met it."

"I've got bigger things to worry about," Fargo said. He turned to Dogan, saw the barrels of the Greener lined on him. "Now?"

"Now," Dogan said.

"Okay," Fargo said, pressed the muzzles into Vane's chest, then whirled, gun pointing at Dogan. "Okay. The game's over."

Dogan's eyes widened. "What?"

Fargo said, "You're covered, Dogan, and if you pull those triggers, you're dead."

Dogan roared, "You bastard! You think you can—?" He closed his fingers on both triggers.

The explosion was tremendous. Fargo was already turning, threatening Jonas and the men behind him with the Fox. But, from the corner of his eye he saw it. The shotgun in Dogan's hands blew up, like a bomb. Its eighteen buckshots blew back, mingled with fragments of the barrels. Dogan's head and upper shoulders dissolved in a red spray. He did not even have time to scream. What was left of him fell limply.

"Vane!" Fargo yelled. "Get my gun and knife out of his belt!" He whirled, menacing paralyzed men with his Fox. They knew he had one round, didn't know there wasn't a second one in the left barrel. Gunhands swooping downward after a frightened second froze. Then Vane came up with a Colt in hand.

"My God," Jonas whispered. "Don't shoot. What happened?" He stared at the bloody thing that once had been Double-Barrel Dogan. It lay on its back, clasping the stock of the double-barreled ten-gauge Greener, the barrels of which had curled back like flowers of steel around his almost severed wrists. Three men, hit by flying buckshot, lay moaning on the ground behind.

Fargo swung the Fox, Vane menaced them with the Colt, and Knight suddenly snatched a rifle from Jonas' paralyzed hands. As if that were a signal, the others moved. Michaelson's big hand chopped a man down, picked up his Marlin. And suddenly it was all over; in shock and confusion, Dogan's men were easy pickings. It had been so long since they'd had a real challenge . . .

Yadkin, coming up with rifle in one hand and pistol in another, snarled, "I'll kill the first bastard moves!"

One man went for his gun. He was in the back ranks, and Fargo didn't see it until his own Colt roared in Vane's hand. A man screamed, collapsed, Colt spilling from his grasp. That stopped them for another moment, and more guns were plucked from holsters, and now Knight strode forward, a gaunt, shambling figure with a rifle in his hand and he said, "All guns. All. Will be thrown out into the center. The first gun, the first . . ." It was as if he were unused to speaking after having been shut up for so long. "The first gun fired and we will kill . . . you all."

Fargo said, "Vane."

"Yes."

"Go inside. Find my bandolier."

Hands were raised as Vane ran into the barroom, came back with Fargo's shell belt. "Now," Fargo said. "Knight, you and the rest of your crew are the weakest, so you get the head start. Down the slot through the side canyon to the boats. Sara will go with you, show you. Sara, move out."

"Yes, oh, yes," Sara said, voice trembling, and she seized a gun. "Come on, Colonel Knight . . ."

"Fargo," Knight said.

"Go with her. We'll be along."

"Yes," Knight answered. "Come on, men." He shambled off behind the girl.

Fargo, facing the cowed men of Dogan's crew said, "All right. You've seen it. You're disarmed, and we've got the whip hand. The first man that follows us is dead."

"Jesus," one man said. "You think we'd try to—"

"Just don't," Fargo said and broke the shotgun and thumbed in another round and closed it and had two more in his hands. "This thing will spray eighteen double-zero and kill a lot of you. I'm a shotgun man and I know what I tell you."

"It ain't worth it," someone said.

"No, it ain't," said Fargo. "But I'll tell you this. The time to clear out of this region is now. Before they box you in. Try Mexico or South America. Don't stay here. There's lots of room yet for people don't want their feet nailed to the floor. All of you," he added. "All of you move out."

They did. He was the rear-guard, with the Fox. Alone.

Alone, and nobody came against him. When Fargo was sure everyone else was in the clear, he backed off. He was very careful as he ran down through the side-canyon's slot to cover his retreat. But no one followed him. He made the sandbar at the mouth of the entrance to Cord's Park. The boats were waiting there, overloaded with men.

"Neal!" Sara's voice was a whisper from the darkness.

Fargo jumped into the lead boat. "Sara, guide us to Lee's Ferry. We're going out there!" Then he picked up a paddle. "Shove off!" he cried, and the boats moved out into the Colorado.

Chapter IX

The Colonel's study in Oyster Bay, Long Island, was decorated with the heads of exotic game: kudu and Cape buffalo from Africa, Kodiak grizzly from the Alaskan coast, jaguar from South America. In a suit, the Colonel looked somehow different as he leaned across his desk.

"Damascus Twist, eh?"

"Yeah," Fargo said.

"Any fool would know it wasn't made for high-powered ammo. Damascus Twist was suitable for the old black powder, muzzle loading or primitive shell guns, but a Damascus Twist barrel will blow sky-high under unusual pressure."

"That's what I figured when I put the corks in," Fargo said.

"The corks?" The Colonel's eyes gleamed.

"Well, he had me. My shotgun and his. And then Sara—Miss Raven here—" Fargo indicated her with a nod of his head, "—thought maybe if she created an upset I had a chance. Guts, pure guts, all the way through. And she did give me a chance. The corks were already there from the whiskey bottles. While Dogan was looking at her, I tamped 'em down both barrels. Clogged up his Greener and hoped it would blow apart. Talked him into giving me back the Fox and . . . It was a long chance, a damned long one, but it all worked out."

The Colonel stared from Fargo to Sara Raven, who now, thanks to Fargo, was dressed in the most fashionable clothes of the time and looked absolutely stunning. "Miss Raven," he said, "I hardly know how to express my thanks." He smiled. "You have helped salvage the scientific results of two expeditions, clear the Colorado for future expeditions and—"

"Try ten thousand dollars," Fargo said.

"What?" The Colonel looked at him, startled.

"I'm pretty well fixed," Fargo said. "But I've got ten thousand coming from you. I want her to have it. What's more, I want her, when I've gone back West, to be welcome here and introduced around. She may not be up on ballroom manners, Colonel, but you can teach her those. And all the rest."

"Yes, of course. We'll welcome her to the bosom of our family . . ."

"Fair enough. Pay her," Fargo said.

The Colonel looked at Fargo, and suddenly he laughed. "Yes. Yes, I understand, now. Of course." He opened the drawer of his desk. Took out a big packet of bills and shoved it toward Sara. "Miss Raven, you'll be a member of our family now."

She stared at the money, stunned. "I never dreamed—"

Fargo said quietly: "There are a lot of things you never dreamed of that you'll see now. Take the money."

"Yes." She put it in her handbag. "Only . . ."

"That's all," Fargo said, touching her shoulder. "You've earned it. Colonel—"

"Yes, Sergeant Fargo?"

"There's a few more things. Vane. Just because he's never been in combat . . . Colonel, that man has guts."

The buckteeth showed in a smile under the wiry mustache. "I've pulled certain strings, Sergeant. Captain Vane has been jumped a rank. He's now Lieutenant-Colonel, and I think his future is assured."

"I should have known you'd be ahead of me. But there's something else."

"What?"

"Give 'em a year or two," Fargo said. "Most aren't real badmen, just cowboys gone wrong. In a couple of years, they'll clear the Colorado and head on to Mexico or South America or Australia . . . Don't send in any more expeditions and push 'em against the wall until then."

The Colonel arose. "They'll have several years. The war in Europe's heating up and the Government's attention is wholly there now. Sooner or later we're bound to be in it . . ."

"Then you'll need 'em," Fargo said. "They'll

come down out of the brakes and join under assumed names and . . . God help the Germans then. Just like in the old days."

"Yes," the Colonel said. "The Rough Riders weren't petunia blossoms!" He laughed, a little wetly. "You're right, Sergeant. If they buy in, God help the Germans. Now . . . my car is waiting outside. It'll take you wherever you want to go. Miss Raven, we'll stay in close touch with you . . ."

"Thank you," she said.

The car was a big Packard limousine. Sara and Fargo got in the tonneau together. "The Waldorf, Manhattan, driver," Fargo said; and the car moved smoothly off.

"Ten thousand dollars," Sara whispered. "Neal, what can I say? I . . . the money is one thing. But you talked as if . . . you're going away again."

"After a while," Fargo said. "In a few weeks. But, don't worry. The Colonel will see to you when I'm gone and make a lady out of you . . ."

"I don't care about being a lady. What I care about is you. Where will you go?"

Fargo stared out the window. "Some place," he said. He felt a certain melancholy. The corks down the shotgun barrel, the Damascus Twist exploding —and now, he would never know. There was no other Double-Barrel Dogan, no other shotgun man of equal rank to pit himself against. It was a shame . . .

Sara's voice brought him back to the present.

"But you will come back?" she asked.

Fargo took out a long, slim, black cigar, bit off its

170

end, clamped it between his teeth. When it was lit, he said:

"I always come back."

THE END

THE TAVERN KNIGHT
Rafael Sabatini

BT51128 $1.75

Historical Adventure

From the author of Scaramouche and Captain Blood!
A swashbuckling novel of revenge, romance, and
rebellion during the English Civil War, of Charles
Stuart and Oliver Cromwell, and of Sir Crispin
Galliard, alias The Tavern Knight, a drunkard,
debauchee, legendary swordsman, and former noble-
man who looks to revenge his murdered family and
regain his usurped title as Lord of Marleigh Hall
by the blade of his sword!

THE PATRIOTS
SEEDS OF REBELLION
Chet Cunningham

BT51129 $1.75

Historical Novel

The embers of rebellion that had been smoldering
now burst into flame with this second part of Belmont Tower's bicenntenial series! Ben Rutledge
had the most to lose . . . he also knew that war was
the only path to total independence. He was prepared
to risk anything.

THE LOVE GODDESS
David Hanna

BT51130 $1.75

Novel

A sizzling novel about one of Hollywood's greatest
stars—tempestuous, violent, sexually obsessed, and
all woman . . . a beautiful woman on a collision
course with triumph . . . and disaster.

THE VIENNA PURSUIT
Anthea Goddard

BT51131 $1.50

Mystery

Marta Fredericks had always believed her father
had been killed by the Nazis. At her mother's death
bed she discovers that he is alive . . . and had been
a Gestapo agent! She begins an adventure that soon
turns to nightmare and carries her from London
to Vienna to a deserted village on the Austro-Hun-
garian border.

BRINGING DOWN THE HOUSE
Richard P. Brickner

BT51139 $1.75
Novel

". . . a wise and delightful book."
—*The New York Times Book Review*

An entrepreneur builds a vast cultural complex in Butte County, South Dakota . . . and into the "heartland of artland" comes a panoply of American artists. Among them is Gregory Lubin, the playwright commissioned to write what he hopes will be Culture City's first *and* last play.

ONE OF OUR BOMBERS IS MISSING
Dan Brennan

BT51140 $1.50
Novel

A searing graphic account of an air mission over Europe in World War II.

". . . one of the best, most moving war novels . . ."
—*Minneapolis Tribune*

"It is a moving salute to the heroes who nightly endure the tension and terrors that are here so graphically described . . . stark honesty and marked artistic skill."
—*Liverpool Evening Express*

THE WIT AND WISDOM OF YOGI BERRA
Phil Pepe

BT51141 $1.50
Sports

"A good book about a good guy."
—*Joe Garagiola*

"Engrossing . . . packed with wildly funny Yogi Berra stories, true and ficticious."
—*Library Journal*

"A very enjoyable and amusing account of one of baseball's truly funny men."
—*Tom Seaver*

SALVATION
BEHIND BARS
Roger Elwood

BT51142 $1.50
Non-fiction

Here are the true stories of men who found their
spiritual salvation while serving prison terms, men
like Charles Colson, ex-advisor to Richard Nixon
... men who would come away from prison with
more than just physical freedom.

TIME OUT OF JOINT
Philip K. Dick

BT51143 $1.25
Science Fiction

A mathematical genius utilizes a vast network of
equations and soon finds that they are out of control
... everything was beginning to go out of its natural
order ... and the world and time were out of joint.

BANDOLERO/FARGO
John Benteen

BT51144 $1.25
Western

Fargo finds himself facing a Mexican firing squad
armed with his own guns and fights a bloody private
war in the middle of the Mexican Revolution.

GHOST AT THE
WEDDING
Elna Stone

BT51145 $1.25
Gothic

Joy turns to nightmare when a young woman discovers her fiance's desire to celebrate a bizarre wed-
ding night ritual ... a ritual that reached out from
the grave and threatened both her sanity and life!

SEND TO: BELMONT TOWER BOOKS
P.O. Box 2301
Norwalk, Connecticut 06852

Please send me the following titles:

Quantity	Book Number	Price
_____	_____	_____
_____	_____	_____
_____	_____	_____
_____	_____	_____

In the event we are out of stock on any of your
selections, please list alternate titles below.

_____	_____	_____
_____	_____	_____
_____	_____	_____
_____	_____	_____

Postage/Handling_____

I enclose . . . . _____

For U.S. orders, add 35¢ per book to cover cost of postage
and handling. Buy five or more copies and we will pay for
shipping. Sorry no C.O.D.'s.
For all other orders, add $1.00 for the first book and 25¢
for each additional title.

☐ Please send me a free catalog.

NAME_____
(Please print)
ADDRESS_____

CITY_____ STATE_____ ZIP_____
Allow Four Weeks for Delivery